NEVER NO MORE

A RANDALL AND CARVER MYSTERY

RANDALL & CARVER MYSTERIES
BOOK 4

BLAIR HOWARD

Cleveland, TN, United States of America
ISBN Print: 979-8-9988024-2-3
www.blairhowardbooks.com
Contact: blairhoward@blairhowardbooks.com

1

'TIL DEATH DO US PART

TUCKER RANDALL GRIPPED THE STEERING WHEEL OF THEIR rented SUV a little tighter than necessary as he navigated the narrow streets of historic St. Augustine. The GPS had guided them off the main highway ten minutes ago, and now they were winding through streets that seemed designed more for horse-drawn carriages than modern vehicles.

"You're being quiet," Mallory said from the passenger seat, studying his profile. "Having second thoughts about this place already?"

"Just concentrating on not scraping the rental against one of these parked cars," Tucker replied, easing around a corner where the street narrowed even further. "Remind me why we didn't just stay at one of those perfectly good beachfront hotels we passed on the way into town?"

Mallory's laugh was light, happy. "Because they were generic chain hotels with no character. The Harrington is historic. It's got stories, atmosphere." She reached across to rest her hand on his knee. "And I thought my husband would appreciate the romance of a Victorian-era hotel by the sea for our honeymoon."

Husband. The word still felt new, strange, but welcome. They'd married less than a week ago, a small ceremony in Chattanooga with just family and close friends. After three years of working together as PI partners, dancing around their feelings, they'd finally made it official. Tucker glanced at Mallory's left hand, the simple gold band catching the Florida sunlight streaming through the windshield. His own matching ring felt foreign on his finger, but not unwelcome.

"D'you think Annie will be okay?" she asked. "We've never been parted from each other this long before."

"Of course she will," Tucker said. "She loves Jen almost as much as she does you. She'll be fine."

"Here it is," Mallory said, pointing ahead. "Oh my God, Tucker, it's perfect."

The Harrington Hotel came into view as they rounded the final corner, and even Tucker had to admit it was impressive. The five-story Victorian structure sat on a bluff overlooking the Atlantic, its white painted wood and wraparound porches gleaming in the February sunlight. Turrets and gables punctuated the roofline, giving the place a fairytale quality that seemed at odds with the modern cars parked in the crushed-shell driveway.

Tucker guided the SUV up the circular drive to the front steps, where a young man in a crisp uniform immediately approached.

"Welcome to the Harrington Hotel," the valet said, opening Mallory's door. "Checking in?"

"Yes," Mallory replied, stepping out and stretching after the long drive from Chattanooga. "The Randall reservation."

"Mr. and Mrs. Randall," the valet said with a smile, glancing at Tucker as he exited the driver's side. "Congratulations on your marriage. We'll get your bags to your room right away. Ms. Harrington likes to personally welcome honeymooners."

As the valet unloaded their luggage from the trunk, Tucker took in the hotel grounds. The property was meticulously maintained, with formal gardens stretching toward the sea cliff edge. Beyond, he could glimpse the Atlantic, blue and vast. A wooden staircase descended the bluff to what appeared to be a private beach area.

"Ms. Harrington?" Tucker asked the valet as he handed over the keys.

"Vivian Harrington," the young man explained, accepting Tucker's tip with a nod. "Owner and manager. The last of the Harrington family line. The hotel's been in her family since 1872."

Mallory's eyes lit up at this snippet of history, and Tucker suppressed a smile. His wife—still strange to think that—had an insatiable curiosity, especially when it came to historical mysteries and cold cases. It was one of the qualities that made her an excellent investigator, even if it sometimes led them into trouble.

"Come on," she said, taking his hand and pulling him toward the wide front steps. "I want to see inside."

The hotel lobby was a step back in time. Original woodwork gleamed with the patina of age and countless polishings. A grand staircase curved upward to the second floor, while Oriental rugs softened the hardwood floors. To their right, a parlor with antique furniture invited guests to sit and relax, while to the left, a small check-in desk was staffed by a young woman in a modern interpretation of Victorian dress.

"Incredible," Mallory murmured, turning slowly to take in the chandelier above them. "Can you imagine how many people have walked through these doors in the last 150 years?"

Before Tucker could respond, a woman's voice cut through the quiet lobby. "And each one with their own story to tell."

They turned to see an elegant woman who Tucker thought to be in her early seventies, approaching from a doorway behind the check-in desk. Her silver hair was pulled back in a neat chignon, and she wore a tailored navy dress that managed to be both classic and current. Her posture was impeccable, and her eyes—sharp and assessing—took in the newlyweds with obvious interest.

"You must be the Randalls," she said, extending a hand first to Mallory, then to Tucker. Her grip was surprisingly firm. "Vivian Harrington. Welcome to my home."

"It's beautiful," Mallory said sincerely. "We're so excited to be here."

"Thank you for having us," Tucker said, noting the way Vivian's gaze lingered on him a moment longer than necessary. There was something calculating in that look that triggered his investigator's instincts, though he couldn't have said why.

"Rebecca will get you checked in," Vivian said, gesturing to the young woman behind the desk. "We've given you our best suite—the Admiral's Quarters. Top floor, corner room with views of both the gardens and the ocean. Once you're settled in, please join us for the welcome reception at five in the main parlor. It's a tradition for our guests to get acquainted on their first evening."

"We'd be delighted," Mallory replied, already moving toward the check-in desk.

As Rebecca processed their registration, Tucker studied the framed photographs adorning the wall behind her. They chronicled the hotel's history—construction photos from the 1870s, various celebrity guests through the decades, and several generations of the Harrington family, culminating in a younger version of Vivian shaking hands with what appeared to be a former president.

"Your room is all ready, Mr. and Mrs. Randall," Rebecca

said, handing them an actual metal key rather than the key cards Tucker had expected. "Fifth floor. The elevator is just past the staircase on the right, or you're welcome to take the stairs if you prefer. Your luggage will be up shortly."

"Thank you," Tucker said, accepting the key. It was heavy, brass, with the room number—501—engraved on a small tag.

As they crossed the lobby toward the elevator, Mallory leaned in close. "Did you see how she looked at you? Like she was trying to figure something out."

Tucker nodded slightly. "I noticed. She was probably just sizing up her new guests. A small hotel like this, the owner probably takes a personal interest."

"Maybe," Mallory said, but her tone said she wasn't entirely convinced. "Or maybe she knows something we don't."

"We've been here all of five minutes," Tucker reminded her with a smile. "Not everything is a mystery to solve, especially not on our honeymoon."

The Admiral's Quarters suite was as impressive as Vivian had said. A spacious sitting room with period furniture opened to a bedroom featuring a king-sized four-poster bed. The bathroom had been modernized without sacrificing the historical character—a claw-foot tub alongside a separate glass-enclosed shower. But the best feature was the pair of French doors leading to a private balcony with a sweeping view of the grounds and the Atlantic beyond.

Mallory immediately went to the doors and stepped outside, breathing in the salt air. Tucker followed, stood behind her, and wrapped his arms around her waist. For a moment, they simply stood together, watching the waves roll in.

"This was a good choice," he admitted, pressing a kiss to her temple. "I'm sorry I grumbled about it."

"You wouldn't be you if you didn't," she replied, leaning

back against his chest. "But I knew you'd come around once you saw it."

A knock at the door announced the arrival of their luggage. Tucker went to the door while Mallory continued to take in the view.

The bellhop—a college-aged young man with a name tag reading "JAMIE"—arranged their bags on the luggage rack. "Is there anything else you need, sir?"

"No, we're all set," Tucker replied, handing him a ten-dollar bill.

"The welcome reception starts at five in the main parlor," Jamie reminded them. "Mr. Blackwood usually gives a brief presentation about the hotel's history. It's actually pretty interesting—especially the bits about the pirate treasure."

That caught Mallory's attention. She turned from the balcony. "Pirate treasure?"

Jamie grinned. "Mr. Blackwood explains it better than I could. He's our historian—knows everything about this place. Stories that would curl your hair." His expression sobered slightly. "Including the darker ones."

"Darker ones?" Mallory pressed, her interest clearly piqued.

"You know, the usual old hotel stuff. Ghost stories, unsolved mysteries, that sort of thing." Jamie shrugged. "Makes for wonderful entertainment." He glanced at his watch. "I should get back downstairs. Enjoy your stay, Mr. and Mrs. Randall."

When the door closed behind him, Tucker turned to find Mallory's eyes gleaming with excitement. "Don't even think about it," he said, recognizing that look all too well. "We're on our honeymoon, Mal. No investigations, no mysteries, no cold cases."

"I didn't say anything," she protested, but her smile gave

her away. "But you have to admit, a historic hotel with pirate treasure and 'darker' mysteries? That's pretty intriguing."

Tucker crossed to her and took her hands in his. "Remember our agreement? Two weeks of just us. No work, no cases."

"I remember," she sighed, then brightened. "But attending a hotel presentation isn't work. It's being social with the other guests. And if the historian happens to mention some fascinating historical details, well, that's just cultural enrichment."

Tucker laughed and pulled her closer. "Fine. Cultural enrichment it is. But if you start taking notes or interviewing staff, I'm hauling you back to the room and keeping you there for the rest of the trip."

Her smile turned mischievous. "Is that a threat or a promise, Mr. Randall?"

"Both," he murmured, lowering his mouth to hers.

THE MAIN PARLOR was even more impressive than the lobby. A grand space with high ceilings, it featured multiple seating areas arranged around two magnificent fireplaces. Although it was Florida in February and quite mild outside, a small fire crackled in one hearth, giving the room a cozy atmosphere as twilight approached. French doors along one wall stood open to the veranda, allowing the sea breeze to filter through.

About a dozen other guests had already gathered when Tucker and Mallory arrived. The hotel staff was circulating with trays of champagne and hors d'oeuvres, creating a festive atmosphere.

Vivian Harrington spotted them immediately and approached, two champagne flutes in hand. "Ah, the

Randalls," she said. "I was wondering if you were going to join us." She offered them each a glass with a knowing smile that made Tucker wonder if the walls of their suite were thinner than they appeared.

"Wouldn't miss it," Mallory replied smoothly, accepting the champagne. "We were just getting… settled in."

"Of course," Vivian said, her eyes twinkling. "Well, allow me to introduce you to some of our other guests." She guided them toward a couple seated near the fireplace. "Walter and Elaine Kincaid," she said. "Walter is a retired federal judge, and they're celebrating their fifth anniversary with us this week."

Judge Kincaid was a distinguished-looking man in his late sixties, with steel-gray hair and the confident bearing of someone accustomed to authority. His wife, Elaine, was significantly younger—mid-thirties at most—with carefully styled blonde hair and a petite figure shown to advantage in a simple but obviously expensive black dress.

"Ah, the newlyweds," Judge Kincaid said, rising to shake their hands. "Vivian mentioned you'd be joining us this week. Congratulations."

"Thank you," Tucker replied. "And congratulations on your anniversary."

"Five years," Elaine said with a slight Southern accent. "Sometimes it feels like just yesterday, sometimes it feels like forever." She patted her husband's hand affectionately, but Tucker noticed her gaze drifted beyond them, scanning the room as if looking for someone.

"What brings you to St. Augustine?" Mallory asked. "Besides celebrating your anniversary, of course."

"Walter has some research to do at the historical archives," Elaine explained. "He's writing his memoirs about his time on the bench, and there's a famous case with connections to this area."

"More specifically, connections to this hotel," Judge Kincaid said. "The Harrington family has quite a... colorful history."

Before he could elaborate, they were interrupted by the arrival of another guest—a striking woman in her fifties with a mane of dark hair streaked with silver. She carried herself with obvious confidence, dressed in flowing layers of jewel-toned silk that said both artistic flair and significant means.

"Ah, Cordelia," Vivian said. "Perfect timing. Let me introduce Tucker and Mallory Randall, our honeymooners. This is Cordelia Winters."

Mallory's eyes widened slightly in recognition. "The mystery novelist?"

Cordelia smiled, clearly pleased to be recognized. "Guilty as charged. Though I prefer to think of myself as a chronicler of human nature under pressure."

"I've read all your books," Mallory said enthusiastically. "The Vanishing Hour is one of my favorites."

"A fan! How lovely," Cordelia said, giving Mallory a more appraising look. "Are you a writer yourself?"

"No, I—"

"My wife and I are private investigators," Tucker said, watching Cordelia's reaction carefully. "Based in Chattanooga."

"Investigators!" Cordelia's interest visibly intensified. "Now that's fascinating. You must have many stories to tell."

"None that would match your imagination, I'm sure," Tucker replied diplomatically.

"Don't be so sure," Cordelia said. "Reality often provides the most bizarre and compelling mysteries. I'd love to pick your brains sometime during your stay. Professional research, you understand."

Mallory looked delighted at the prospect, but before she could respond, a man's voice called for everyone's attention.

The crowd quieted as all eyes turned to a middle-aged man standing near the unlit fireplace at the far end of the parlor.

"Good evening, ladies and gentlemen," he said, his voice carrying easily across the room. "For our new arrivals, I'm Edwin Blackwood, the Harrington Hotel's historian and archivist. It's our tradition here to share a bit of the hotel's colorful past during our welcome reception."

Edwin Blackwood was a lean man of about sixty, with thinning brown hair and wire-rimmed glasses that gave him a scholarly appearance. He wore a tweed jacket despite the Florida climate, completing the stereotype of an academic.

"The Harrington has stood on this bluff since 1872," Blackwood continued, "built by Captain James Harrington after he made his fortune in shipping following the Civil War." He gestured to a portrait above the mantel—a stern-faced man with an impressive beard and penetrating eyes. "The Captain, as he was known even after retiring from the sea, had a reputation for shrewdness in business and an eye for opportunity."

Blackwood launched into a well-practiced narrative of the hotel's early days, describing famous guests and notable events. Tucker found his attention wandering until the historian's tone shifted subtly.

"Of course, not all of the Harrington's history is so… celebratory," Blackwood said, his voice lowering dramatically. "Like many historic properties, we have our share of tragedies and mysteries."

Now he had Mallory's complete attention. Tucker could practically feel her interest radiating as she leaned forward slightly.

"Many of you have heard rumors of treasure associated with the Harrington," Blackwood continued. "While the most sensational stories of pirate gold are likely apocryphal, there is compelling evidence that Spanish colonial artifacts of significant value may be hidden somewhere on the property."

A murmur ran through the assembled guests. Tucker noticed Judge Kincaid and his wife exchange a significant look, while across the room, a man Tucker hadn't met yet—middle-aged with an expensive haircut and a too-deep tan—seemed to be taking mental notes.

"Captain Harrington was known to have acquired several rare items from Spanish shipwrecks," Blackwood explained. "Items that disappeared after his death in 1889. His son, Thomas Harrington, claimed his father had hidden them somewhere on the property, along with documents of historical significance. To this day, they've never been found."

"Despite many people looking," Vivian Harrington interjected smoothly, stepping forward to stand beside Blackwood. "Including quite a few unauthorized treasure hunters over the years." Her tone was light, but Tucker detected a warning beneath the surface.

"Indeed," Blackwood acknowledged with a slight nod. "But perhaps the hotel's most notorious mystery involves a more recent tragedy. Forty years ago, in February 1985, a young maid named Isabella Cruz was found dead on the hotel grounds. Her death was ruled a homicide, but the case was never solved."

Another murmur, this one carrying a distinct note of unease. Tucker noticed an elderly woman—Hispanic, wearing a housekeeper's uniform—slip quietly from the room, her expression troubled.

"The circumstances were particularly mysterious," Blackwood continued, clearly warming to his subject. "Cruz had worked at the hotel for several years without incident. Then, during renovations to the east wing, she apparently discovered something that cost her her life. What that something was has remained a mystery for half a century."

"I think that's enough grim history for a welcome reception, Edwin," Vivian interrupted, her smile now sadly forced. "Our guests came for relaxation, not true crime stories."

"Of course," Blackwood said, though he didn't look pleased at being cut off. "My apologies. Let me end on a more pleasant note. The Harrington has hosted five presidents, countless celebrities, and even royalty over its 150-year history. We're delighted to add all of you to our distinguished guest list. Please enjoy your stay—and if you'd like to hear more about our history, I lead tours of the property every morning at ten."

As the formal presentation progressed, guests broke into smaller conversation groups. Tucker felt Mallory's hand slip into his.

"We're definitely taking that tour tomorrow," she whispered.

Tucker sighed, knowing resistance was futile. "Cultural enrichment?"

"Exactly," she said with a grin. "Plus, did you see how Vivian cut him off when he started talking about the murdered maid? There's definitely a story there."

Before Tucker could respond, they were approached by the well-dressed man with the deep tan who'd been so interested in Blackwood's mention of treasure.

"Gregory Marsh," he introduced himself, extending a manicured hand. "Antiques dealer. I couldn't help overhearing that you two are private investigators. Fascinating profession."

"On vacation," Tucker emphasized, shaking the man's hand briefly.

"Of course, of course," Marsh said with a smile that didn't reach his eyes. "Still, I imagine you never really turn off that investigative instinct. I wonder what you make of Blackwood's treasure stories?"

"We haven't formed an opinion," Tucker replied neutrally. "We just arrived today."

"Well, I've been coming to the Harrington for years," Marsh said, lowering his voice conspiratorially. "Between us, Blackwood's not just spinning tales for the tourists. There really is something valuable hidden here—something the Harrington family has been keeping secret for generations."

Mallory's interest was clearly piqued. "What makes you so sure?"

Marsh glanced around, then leaned in closer. "Let's just say I've seen documentation that very few people have access to. Historical records that suggest Captain Harrington recovered items from a Spanish galleon that would be worth millions today."

"That sounds like quite a story," Tucker said noncommittally.

"More than a story," Marsh insisted. "And February is a significant month in the hotel's history. Did you notice Blackwood mentioned the maid was killed in February, 1985? Exactly forty years ago this month. Coincidence?" He raised an eyebrow dramatically.

Before either Tucker or Mallory could respond, Vivian Harrington materialized at their side. "Mr. Marsh," she said coolly, "I hope you're not bending our newlyweds' ears with your theories."

"Just making conversation, Vivian," Marsh replied with a smile that seemed designed to irritate. "Sharing my appreciation for the hotel's fascinating history."

"How thoughtful," Vivian replied, not bothering to hide her sarcasm. "However, I need to borrow the Randalls to introduce them to some of our other guests."

As Vivian led them away, Mallory glanced back at Marsh, who raised his champagne glass in a mock toast.

"I apologize for Gregory," Vivian said once they were out

of earshot. "He fancies himself something of an expert on the hotel's history, but his theories are... fanciful at best."

"He seems very convinced about the treasure," Tucker said.

Vivian sighed. "The Harrington has always attracted treasure hunters and conspiracy theorists. My family has learned to tolerate them as long as they don't start digging up the garden or knocking holes in the walls." She paused, studying them both. "But you two aren't the treasure-hunting types, are you? Private investigators, I understand?"

"On vacation," Tucker emphasized again.

"Of course," Vivian said, in much the same tone Marsh had used. "Well, I hope you enjoy your stay with us. St. Augustine is full of history and romance—perfect for a honeymoon." She glanced across the room and frowned slightly. "If you'll excuse me, I need to check on something in the kitchen. Please, enjoy the reception."

As Vivian departed, Mallory turned to Tucker with eyes bright with excitement. "Did you hear all that? A forty-year-old unsolved murder, rumors of hidden treasure, and it's all connected to February somehow."

"What happened to 'cultural enrichment'?" Tucker asked dryly.

"This is way beyond cultural enrichment," Mallory replied, practically bouncing on her toes. "This is a real historical mystery! And everyone here seems to have their own theory about it."

Tucker took a sip of his champagne, surveying the room. Judge Kincaid was now deep in conversation with Blackwood near one of the bookcases. Elaine Kincaid stood nearby, though her attention seemed divided between her husband and Gregory Marsh, who had moved to chat with Cordelia Winters by the French doors.

"You know," Tucker said thoughtfully, "for a small hotel, there are a lot of people interested in its secrets."

"Exactly," Mallory said eagerly. "Doesn't that strike you as odd? A retired judge who's specifically researching this hotel's history, a mystery novelist, an antiques dealer obsessed with hidden treasure… and our host, who seems very keen to downplay certain aspects of the past."

Despite himself, Tucker felt his investigator's instincts stirring. The collection of personalities seemed unusually focused on the hotel's secrets. But before he could pursue that thought, a hotel staff member approached with a tray of hors d'oeuvres, temporarily distracting Mallory.

As Tucker watched his wife—still strange but wonderful to think of her that way—chatting animatedly with the server, he couldn't shake the feeling that their honeymoon was about to become significantly more complicated than he'd anticipated. Mallory had that look in her eyes, the one that meant she'd found a mystery she couldn't resist.

So much for two weeks of relaxation.

2

A TOAST TO THE PAST

THE WELCOME RECEPTION CONTINUED WELL INTO THE evening, with Mallory making it a point to circulate and chat with as many guests as possible. Tucker recognized her investigative technique—casual conversation that subtly probed for information—and resigned himself to the fact that their honeymoon had already morphed into something else entirely. At least she was enjoying herself, her eyes bright with the thrill of potential discovery.

Tucker maintained a more reserved approach, watching the interactions around the room with the detached observation he'd honed during his FBI years. The dynamics were interesting: Judge Kincaid dominated whatever conversation he joined, while his young wife, Elaine, seemed to float between social groups, charming and attentive but somehow always managing to steer the discussions toward the hotel's history.

Gregory Marsh, the antiques dealer, had cornered Edwin Blackwood by one of the bookcases, their conversation animated but hushed. Vivian Harrington moved silently around the room, the consummate hostess, but Tucker noticed how she regularly positioned herself within earshot of Blackwood and Marsh.

"Making new friends?" Tucker asked as Mallory rejoined him near the French doors leading to the veranda.

"Better than that," she replied quietly, her expression alight with excitement. "Making connections. Did you know that before she married the judge, Elaine Kincaid used to work for an antiquities hunter? And Cordelia Winters was researching a book about Spanish colonial treasure when she agreed to stay here."

Tucker raised an eyebrow. "You learned all that in the space of what, forty-five minutes?"

"People like to talk," Mallory shrugged, helping herself to a stuffed mushroom from a passing tray. "Especially when you show genuine interest. Oh, and the chef—Pierre Dupont —has been with the hotel for seven years and apparently has an extensive collection of colonial artifacts himself."

"Let me guess," Tucker said dryly. "You've already arranged a tour of the kitchen."

Mallory grinned. "Tomorrow afternoon. I told him we're both fascinated by historical cooking methods."

"Of course you did." Tucker shook his head, unable to completely suppress his smile. Mallory's enthusiasm was infectious, even when it derailed their plans. "Remind me again what happened to our agreement about no investigations during our honeymoon?"

"This isn't an investigation," Mallory protested, though her eyes danced with mischief. "It's just... getting to know our fellow guests. Making conversation. Being sociable."

"Right," Tucker said skeptically. "And I suppose your notebook is already filled with observations and questions?"

"I haven't written anything down," she countered, then said under her breath, "yet."

Tucker might have pressed the point, but they were interrupted by the arrival of Cordelia Winters, who approached with two fresh glasses of champagne.

"I thought you might need a refill," she said, handing them each a glass. "And I wanted to continue our conversation about your investigative work. It's not often I get to speak with real detectives."

"We're hardly detectives in the traditional sense," Tucker clarified. "Private investigators focus more on surveillance, background checks, locating missing persons—"

"And occasionally solving murders that local police can't crack," Mallory interjected proudly. "My niece Julie was murdered three years ago. That's actually how Tucker and I started working together."

Cordelia's eyes widened with interest. "How tragic—and fascinating. Was it a particularly complex case?"

"It had its challenges," Tucker admitted, uncomfortable with the direction of the conversation but unwilling to cut Mallory off when she spoke about Julie. The case remained deeply personal for her and solving it had been the foundation of both their professional partnership and private partnership.

"The local police had essentially given up," Mallory explained. "They had a suspect—my niece's boyfriend—but not enough evidence to charge him. Tucker was reluctant to get involved at first." She smiled at the memory. "He's a bit of a lone wolf."

"Was," Tucker corrected with a thin smile. "Things change."

"Indeed, they do," Cordelia said, glancing between them with obvious interest. "And now you're married. Life has a way of surprising us, doesn't it? One moment you're on one path and then circumstances conspire to set you on an entirely different journey."

Something in her tone made Tucker study her more carefully. "You sound like you speak from experience."

Cordelia took a sip of her champagne before answering. "Let's just say my current project is somewhat personal. I've been researching the Spanish treasure fleet of 1715 for my next novel—a historical mystery. The Harrington Hotel's connection to that history is… significant to me."

"Because of the rumored treasure?" Mallory asked.

"Among other things," Cordelia replied enigmatically. "The truth is always more complex than the stories we tell ourselves, don't you find?"

Before either could respond, the conversation was interrupted by the sound of glass breaking, followed by raised voices from across the room. All heads turned to see Gregory Marsh and Edwin Blackwood facing off near the bookshelves, a shattered champagne flute at their feet.

"That document belongs to the hotel archives!" Blackwood was saying, his scholarly demeanor replaced by obvious anger. "You had no right to even touch it, let alone make copies."

"It was in the public library's collection," Marsh countered, his tan face flushed. "Public domain, Edwin. I've already authenticated it with experts at the University of Florida."

"What document?" Mallory whispered to Cordelia, who was watching the confrontation with undisguised interest.

"Captain Harrington's journal, I imagine," Cordelia murmured back. "There's supposedly a missing volume that contains clues to where he hid his… acquisitions from the 1715 fleet."

Vivian Harrington had already swooped in, placing herself between the two men with the practiced ease of someone accustomed to defusing tensions.

"Gentlemen, please," she said, her voice carrying enough

authority to silence them both. "This is hardly the venue for academic disputes. Our guests are here to relax, not witness arguments over historical minutiae."

"Minutiae?" Blackwood sputtered. "Vivian, he's claiming to have found—"

"We can discuss this tomorrow," Vivian cut him off firmly. "In private. For now, I think it's best if we all remember our manners."

The tension in the room was palpable. Tucker watched as Judge Kincaid observed the confrontation with calculating interest, while his wife Elaine seemed to be suppressing a smile behind her champagne glass.

"Well," Cordelia said into the awkward silence that followed. "I believe I'll step outside for some fresh air. Care to join me?" she asked, looking at Tucker and Mallory.

The veranda overlooked the hotel gardens, which were artfully lit with subtle landscape lighting. The sound of the ocean provided a soothing backdrop as they settled into a grouping of wicker chairs. The February evening was mild, with just enough chill in the air to make Mallory draw her light wrap more closely around her shoulders.

"That was dramatic," Mallory said once they were seated. "Does that sort of thing happen often here?"

Cordelia laughed lightly. "The Harrington seems to bring out powerful emotions in people. Especially those interested in its secrets."

"And you're one of those people," Tucker said.

"Guilty as charged," Cordelia admitted. "But my interest is primarily literary. Gregory Marsh, on the other hand... he's been trying to get his hands on the Harrington artifacts for years. Rumor has it he has a wealthy client who's obsessed with the 1715 fleet and will pay virtually any price for authenticated items."

"And Blackwood?" Mallory asked. "Where does he fit in?"

"Edwin sees himself as the guardian of the Harrington's history," Cordelia explained. "He's been the hotel historian for over twenty years, completely devoted to preserving its legacy. Some say a bit too devoted." She lowered her voice, though they were alone on the veranda. "He lives in a cottage on the property and rarely leaves the grounds. Spends most of his time in the archives, cataloging and researching."

Tucker filed this information away, noting how freely Cordelia shared what she knew. Either she was naturally forthcoming, or she had reasons of her own for wanting them to know these details.

"And what about the murdered maid Blackwood mentioned?" Mallory asked, getting to the question Tucker knew had been burning in her mind since the presentation. "Isabella Cruz, right? What's her connection to all this?"

Cordelia's expression grew more serious. "Ah, poor Isabella. That's a dark chapter in the hotel's history, one that Vivian would prefer stayed buried." She glanced toward the French doors, as if to ensure they weren't being overheard. "The official story is that she was killed by an intruder—a robbery gone wrong. But there have always been whispers she discovered something during the renovations. Something related to the Harrington treasure."

"After forty years, you'd think any evidence would be long gone," Tucker commented.

"Physical evidence, perhaps," Cordelia said. "But memories linger, especially in small communities like this. The head housekeeper, Gloria Mendez, worked here back then. She was friends with Isabella. And the gardener, Francisco Ruiz, is Isabella's cousin. Neither of them ever believed the intruder story."

"Are they still working here?" Mallory asked, her investigative instincts clearly engaged.

"Gloria is. You might have noticed her at the reception—

the elderly Hispanic woman. She left when Blackwood started talking about Isabella. Francisco still tends the gardens, though he must be in his late seventies by now. They're the only staff members who've been here since before Vivian took over management of the hotel."

Tucker caught Mallory's expression, recognizing the familiar look that meant she was already planning how to approach these potential witnesses. Before she could ask more questions, however, they were joined on the veranda by Judge Kincaid and his wife.

"Ah, the famous novelist holding court," the judge said congenially as they approached. "Mind if we join you? That discussion inside was becoming rather tedious."

"By all means," Cordelia replied, though Tucker detected a slight stiffening in her posture.

The judge settled his substantial frame into one of the wicker chairs, which creaked in protest. Elaine remained standing, her hand resting lightly on her husband's shoulder.

"I was just telling the Randalls about some of the hotel's interesting history," Cordelia explained.

"Fascinating place, isn't it?" Judge Kincaid said, his tone suggesting he was about to deliver a lecture. "I've been studying the legal history of this property for my memoirs. Did you know that Captain James Harrington was involved in a significant Supreme Court case in 1879? It established important precedent regarding salvage rights for shipwrecks."

"I didn't," Tucker admitted, genuinely interested despite himself.

"It's how he legally acquired many of the Spanish artifacts that are supposedly hidden somewhere on the grounds," the judge continued. "Though whether they're still here is another question entirely. My research suggests they may have been moved decades ago."

Elaine's hand tightened visibly on her husband's shoulder. "Walter, darling, I'm sure the newlyweds don't want a legal history lesson on their first night."

"On the contrary," Mallory said quickly. "I find it fascinating. Especially if it connects to the murdered maid Blackwood mentioned."

Judge Kincaid's bushy eyebrows rose. "Isabella Cruz? Now that's an interesting cold case. I've reviewed the original police reports as part of my research. Shoddy police work, if you ask me. Classic tunnel vision—fixating on the intruder theory to the exclusion of all other possibilities."

"What other possibilities were there?" Tucker asked, his own professional interest piqued.

The judge leaned forward, lowering his voice conspiratorially. "Well, Cruz was found near the east wing renovation site, where workers had opened up a section of wall that hadn't been accessed in decades. According to witness statements that were largely ignored, she'd been seen carrying something from that area just days before her death. Something small but apparently valuable enough to kill for."

"Walter," Elaine said, her voice carrying a warning note. "Remember what happened the last time you discussed this case in public?"

The judge waved a dismissive hand. "That was different. Mr. Blackwood took personal offense, because he believes his version of the hotel's history is the only valid one." He turned back to Tucker and Mallory. "The truth is, there are powerful people in this community who would prefer certain aspects of the Harrington's past remain buried. Figuratively speaking, of course."

Tucker noticed Cordelia watching this exchange with intense interest, her fingers absently turning her champagne glass. "And your research," he asked the judge, "is it focused primarily on the legal aspects, or are you interested in the treasure angle as well?"

"A bit of both," Judge Kincaid admitted. "The legal precedents are what drew me initially, but I must confess, the mystery of what happened to those artifacts is compelling. If they were indeed moved, the question becomes by whom and to where?" He smiled, though the expression didn't reach his eyes. "And more importantly, who stands to benefit from keeping their location secret after all these years?"

Elaine checked her watch, a delicate gold piece that caught the light. "Darling, it's getting late, and you have that early call with your publisher tomorrow."

The judge sighed but nodded. "My wife, ever mindful of my schedule." He pushed himself to his feet with the deliberate movements of a man accustomed to commanding respect. "A pleasure chatting with you all. Perhaps we can continue this discussion another time."

As they departed, Cordelia waited until they were out of earshot before murmuring, "Interesting that the judge is so fixated on Isabella Cruz's murder after forty years."

"Not just the murder," Mallory pointed out. "The treasure too. Everyone here seems obsessed with it."

"With good reason," Cordelia replied. "If the stories are true, the artifacts Captain Harrington salvaged would be worth millions in today's market. Historical value aside, the pure gold content alone would be substantial."

Tucker glanced through the French doors to where Edwin Blackwood was now engaged in conversation with Vivian Harrington, their body language suggesting a disagreement conducted in hushed tones.

"And Blackwood?" he asked. "Where does his interest lie? Purely academic?"

Cordelia followed his gaze. "That's the question, isn't it? Edwin presents himself as the guardian of the Harrington's historical integrity, but he's been searching for those artifacts himself for twenty years. Some say he's found documents that provide clues to their location, but has kept them hidden from Vivian."

"Why would he do that?" Mallory asked.

"Control, perhaps," Cordelia said. "Or maybe he believes they rightfully belong to the historical record, not to the Harrington family. He and Vivian have had a... complex relationship over the years."

Tucker saw how Cordelia emphasized the word "complex" and filed that observation away for later consideration. The author clearly knew more than she was sharing.

"Well," Cordelia said, draining the last of her champagne. "This has been delightful, but I should retire for the evening. I have an early writing session planned for tomorrow." She rose gracefully from her chair. "I hope we'll continue our conversation during your stay. I find you both... refreshingly perceptive."

After she left, Tucker and Mallory remained on the veranda, the sounds of the reception gradually diminishing as other guests began to depart as well.

"So," Tucker said finally. "Still think this is just 'cultural enrichment'?"

Mallory's eyes sparkled in the subtle landscape lighting. "Okay, you were right. Something unusual is happening beyond typical hotel ghost stories. A forty-year-old unsolved murder, missing treasure, guests with suspicious interests in both... it's like we walked into one of Cordelia's novels."

"Complete with a suspicious hotel owner, a passionate historian, and various other colorful characters," Tucker said. "All that's missing is Hercule Poirot. The question is, though, what do we do about it? This is supposed to be our honeymoon, Mal."

Mallory leaned over and took his hand. "It still is. But you have to admit, you're intrigued too. I saw your expression when the judge was talking about the old case. That was your 'something doesn't add up' face."

Tucker couldn't deny it. His investigator's instincts had been thoroughly engaged by the evening's revelations. "Alright," he said. "I'll admit I'm curious. But let's not forget why we're here. We've waited a long time for this trip."

"We can do both," Mallory insisted. "Enjoy our honeymoon and maybe casually look into a historical mystery. Think of it as... a couple's activity."

Tucker laughed despite himself. "Only you would consider an unsolved murder 'a couple's activity.'"

"It's how we met," she reminded him with a smile. "And besides, we're not actively investigating anything. Just... listening. Observing. Maybe asking a few questions."

"Right," Tucker said, recognizing the familiar pattern. This was exactly how Mallory had drawn him into at least a half-dozen cases he could think of: just a few questions, just gathering information, just following her intuition until suddenly they were neck-deep in a murder investigation.

But he had to admit, there was something about the Harrington Hotel's mysteries that called to him as well. The connections between the past and present, the way old secrets seemed to be surfacing after forty years, the unusual collection of people who had gathered here in February 2025, exactly forty years after Isabella Cruz's murder... it all pointed to a convergence that couldn't be mere coincidence.

"Fine," he said finally. "We can ask a few questions. But," he held up a finger as Mallory's face lit up, "we maintain perspective. This is still our honeymoon. Any... unofficial inquiries take second place to enjoying our time together. Deal?"

"Deal," Mallory said quickly, sealing it with a kiss that said she had her own ideas about enjoying their time together.

When she pulled back, she said, "And I promise not to bring my notebook to the beach."

"That's a start," Tucker said dryly.

As they made their way back through the now nearly empty parlor, Tucker noticed Edwin Blackwood gathering his notes from the earlier presentation. The historian looked troubled, his earlier confidence replaced by a furrowed brow and distracted manner.

"Mr. Blackwood," Mallory called, never one to miss an opportunity. "Your presentation was fascinating. We'd love to join your tour tomorrow morning, if that's alright."

Blackwood looked up, seeming to need a moment to place them. "Ah, the newlyweds. Of course, the tour starts at ten from the front lobby." He hesitated, then said in a lower voice, "If you're particularly interested in the hotel's history, I could show you some of the archive materials afterward. Items not included in the general tour."

"We'd like that," Mallory said before Tucker could respond.

Blackwood nodded, glancing over his shoulder toward where Vivian Harrington was speaking with the hotel staff. "Good. And if I might suggest... discretion. Ms. Harrington prefers that certain aspects of the hotel's past remain... curated for general consumption."

With that cryptic comment, he collected his materials and departed through a side door, leaving Tucker and Mallory to exchange significant looks.

"Curiouser and curiouser," Mallory murmured as they headed for the staircase.

Tucker couldn't help but agree. Their honeymoon had just become considerably more intriguing than either of them had anticipated.

3

MORNING TIDE

MALLORY WOKE BEFORE DAWN, DRAWN FROM SLEEP BY THE distant sound of waves. For a moment, she lay still, orienting herself in the unfamiliar room. Beside her, Tucker slept soundly, his breathing deep and even. The digital clock on the nightstand read 5:47 AM.

Sleep wouldn't return, she knew that much. Once her mind engaged, especially with a potential mystery to unravel, rest became impossible. Carefully, she slipped from beneath the covers and went to the French doors that led out to their private balcony. Drawing aside the heavy curtain, she peered out at the predawn world.

The sky was just beginning to lighten, a thin line of pale gray separating the ocean from the darkness above. The tide was out, revealing a wide expanse of wet sand. *Perfect for an early morning walk*, she thought. Tucker wouldn't be up for at least another hour, and she'd never been good at lying in bed waiting for the day to begin.

She dressed quickly in jeans and a light sweater, scribbling a note for Tucker in case he woke while she was gone: "Gone for a walk along the beach. Back by 7. Love, M."

The hotel was silent as she made her way downstairs, her footsteps muffled by the thick carpeting. The night clerk at the front desk gave her a friendly nod as she passed, but otherwise, the grand lobby was deserted. Outside, the air was cool and fresh, carrying the tang of salt and seaweed. Mallory took a deep breath, feeling invigorated as she followed the path that led to the wooden staircase descending the bluff.

The stairs creaked slightly beneath her weight, weathered by years of exposure to the elements. At the bottom, the beach stretched in both directions, pristine and empty in the early morning light. To her left, the shore curved gently toward a series of tide pools formed by an outcropping of rocks. To her right, the sand extended toward the public beach access point, still too far away to see any other early risers.

Mallory turned left, drawn to the rocky promontory. The tide was low enough that she could walk around it rather than over it, and she was curious to see what marine life might be visible in the pools. As she approached, the growing light revealed the rocky formation in more detail—a jumble of boulders and smaller stones that had likely broken off from the bluff over decades of erosion.

Something caught her eye as she drew closer—an unusual shape among the rocks, something that didn't belong in the natural formation. She quickened her pace, her investigator's instincts already on alert.

What she had initially taken for a piece of driftwood was, in fact, a human figure, facedown in one of the larger tide pools. The body was clothed in dark pants and what looked like a tweed jacket, now soaked through. Gray hair floated gently in the shallow water, moving with the subtle current.

Mallory's heart pounded as she scrambled over the smaller rocks to reach the pool. Though she already suspected what she would find, training and instinct kicked in. She knelt beside the pool and reached for the person's wrist, searching for a pulse she knew wouldn't be there. The skin was cold, the body already stiff. This person had been dead for hours.

Carefully, she leaned forward to see the face, confirming what she had already guessed from the distinctive tweed jacket. Edwin Blackwood, the hotel historian, lay dead in the tide pool, his glasses still perched incongruously on his nose, his eyes open and fixed in an expression of surprise.

"Damn," Mallory whispered, pulling her hand back. Her mind raced through the possibilities. Had he fallen from the bluff above? An accident during a late-night walk? But as she shifted position to look more carefully, she noticed something that sent a chill through her that had nothing to do with the morning air—distinct bruising around Blackwood's neck, partially hidden by his collar but visible now that she was looking for it.

This was no accidental fall. Someone had strangled Edwin Blackwood and then placed or pushed his body into the tide pool, perhaps hoping the incoming tide would carry him out to sea. If she hadn't happened to walk this way at low tide, that might well have happened.

Mallory stood, scanning the beach and bluff above. She was alone, as far as she could tell, but she couldn't shake the feeling of being watched. She needed to report this immediately and get back to Tucker. Pulling her phone from her pocket, she was unsurprised to find no signal. The bluff likely blocked reception from the nearest tower.

With one last glance at Blackwood's body, she began making her way back toward the hotel stairs, moving as quickly as she could while still scanning the beach for any evidence—footprints, dropped items, anything that might indicate who had been here last night. The sand near the tide pools was too rocky to hold clear impressions, but as she moved toward the stairs, she noticed what looked like multiple sets of footprints leading from the base of the steps to the rocky area.

The tracks were partially degraded, likely from the previous night, and impossible to clearly distinguish individual patterns. Still, it said that someone—perhaps more than one person—had walked this same path hours earlier. Whether those tracks belonged to Blackwood and his killer was impossible to tell without proper forensic examination.

Climbing the stairs quickly, Mallory reached the hotel grounds and immediately headed for the front entrance. As she crossed the manicured lawn, she noticed a light on in a small cottage set back among the trees—probably Blackwood's residence, based on what Cordelia had told them. Had he left that light on himself, or had someone been in his home after his death?

The night clerk looked up in surprise as Mallory burst through the front doors.

"I need to use your phone," she said urgently. "There's a body on the beach—Edwin Blackwood. It looks like he's been murdered."

The young man's eyes widened in shock. "Mr. Blackwood? Are you sure?"

"Positive," Mallory said. "I need to call the police immediately. And I need to get back to my room to wake my husband."

The clerk fumbled for the phone with shaking hands. "Should I… should I wake Ms. Harrington?"

"Yes, but I need to call the police first," Mallory said, holding out her hand as the clerk dialed 911.

She took the phone, made her report, including her personal details, handed the phone back to the clerk, and ran to the stairs, unwilling to wait for the elevator.

"Tell Ms. Harrington what's happened," she yelled over her shoulder, 'and that the police are on their way."

She took the stairs two at a time, adrenaline carrying her up five flights without pause. In their suite, she found Tucker already awake, reading her note with a furrowed brow.

"There you are," he began, but his expression changed immediately upon seeing her face. "What's happened?"

"Edwin Blackwood," she said, still catching her breath. "Dead in the tide pool below the hotel. Strangled from the looks of it, then placed in the water. I found him during my walk."

"What?" Tucker was stunned. "You're sure he's dead?"

She gave him the look. "Of course I am. He was strangled. There's bruising around the neck. And the body position; it doesn't match that of someone who fell from the clifftop. He was deliberately placed in that tide pool."

Tucker was already pulling on clothes. "Police?"

"I called them, and I told the clerk to wake Vivian."

Tucker nodded, tying his shoes. "What time did you find him?"

"About fifteen minutes ago, around 6:15. He's been dead for hours—rigor had set in."

"So, sometime between ten and midnight," Tucker said. "Did you notice anything else? Footprints, evidence?"

"There were multiple sets of footprints from the stairs to the tide pools, but they were degraded—probably from last night. And Blackwood's cottage has a light on."

Tucker finished dressing and reached for his jacket. "Let's head downstairs. The police will want to talk to you."

The lobby was a flurry of activity. Vivian Harrington stood near the front desk in a silk robe hastily thrown over pajamas, her silver hair loose around her shoulders, making her look older and more vulnerable than she had the previous evening. She was issuing rapid instructions to several staff members who had apparently been summoned from their quarters.

She broke off when she saw Tucker and Mallory approach. "Is it true?" she demanded, her voice tight with tension. "Edwin is dead? Murdered?"

"I'm afraid so, yes," Mallory replied. "I found his body in the tide pool below the hotel."

Vivian closed her eyes briefly, her composure wavering. "Dear God. Not again."

The slip was slight, but revealing. But before either Tucker or Mallory could question it, the front doors opened to admit a tall, broad-shouldered man with deep-set eyes and the unmistakable bearing of law enforcement. He was followed by two uniformed officers, who immediately began scanning the lobby.

"Detective Diego Santos, St. Augustine Police," the man introduced himself, flashing a badge. "I understand there's been a death?"

"I found the body." Mallory stepped forward. "Mallory Randall. This is my husband, Tucker."

Detective Santos assessed them both with a quick glance. "You're guests here?"

"Honeymooners," Tucker supplied. "My wife went for an early morning walk and discovered Blackwood's body in the tide pools."

"And you are?" Santos asked, turning to Vivian.

"Vivian Harrington. I own the hotel. Edwin Blackwood was our historian and a... dear friend." Her voice caught slightly on the last words. "This is a terrible tragedy."

Santos nodded, his expression giving nothing away. "Mrs. Randall, I'll need you to show us exactly where you found the body. Mr. Randall, if you could wait here, Officer Rivera will take your statement."

Tucker caught Mallory's eye, a silent communication

passing between them—she would observe everything she could while with the detective, and they would compare notes later.

"Actually," Tucker said, producing his old FBI credentials from his wallet, "I was a special agent with the Bureau for eight years. I might be able to assist."

Santos examined the credentials with a flicker of surprise. "Former Bureau? What brings you to St. Augustine?"

"As I said, we're on our honeymoon," Tucker repeated. "But I'm happy to offer any professional assistance if needed."

The detective seemed to weigh this offer before responding. "I appreciate the gesture, Mr. Randall, but we can handle this. But as a professional courtesy, I'll keep you informed of anything relevant to your stay here." His tone made it clear this was as far as his cooperation would extend.

Mallory suppressed a smile. She knew Tucker well enough to recognize that the detective's dismissal would only sharpen his interest. Nothing motivated her husband like being told to stay out of something.

"Of course," Tucker said smoothly. "We're just here to enjoy our honeymoon."

Santos turned back to Mallory. "Mrs. Randall, if you'll come with me? I need you to walk me through exactly what you saw and did this morning."

As Mallory followed Santos and his officers toward the beach access, she glanced back to see Tucker already engaged in conversation with Vivian Harrington, his expression neutral but his posture attentive. He was in information-gathering mode, and Vivian, in her distressed state, would likely reveal more than she intended.

The beach looked different now in the full morning light, the peaceful solitude disturbed by the presence of police officers setting up a perimeter around the tide pools. Santos walked beside Mallory in silence until they reached the edge of the rocky area.

"Stay here," he instructed, ducking under the police tape his officers had already strung. He approached the pool where Blackwood's body lay, crouching to examine it without touching anything. After a moment, he rejoined Mallory.

"Walk me through exactly what happened this morning," he said, pulling out a small notebook.

Mallory recounted her early walk, the discovery of the body, and her observations about the bruising and the footprints.

"And you're certain about the bruising?" Santos asked, making notes. "You have medical training?"

"No," Mallory admitted. "But my husband and I are private investigators. I've worked enough cases to recognize signs of strangulation."

Santos looked up sharply. "Private investigators? You didn't mention that."

"You didn't ask about our professions," Mallory pointed out. "We're here on our honeymoon, not professionally."

The detective studied her for a moment, his expression unreadable. "You and your FBI husband just happened to be staying at a hotel where a murder occurs. That's quite a coincidence."

"We arrived yesterday," Mallory said, meeting his gaze steadily. "We'd never met Edwin Blackwood before the welcome reception last night. Feel free to verify our travel arrangements."

Santos made another note. "And what was your impression of Mr. Blackwood during this reception?"

"He seemed knowledgeable and passionate about the hotel's history," Mallory replied. "He had some kind of disagreement with another guest—Gregory Marsh, an antiques dealer—about hotel documents. It got heated enough that Vivian had to intervene."

"What kind of documents?"

"Something about a journal, I think. Marsh claimed he'd found it in the public library and had it authenticated by experts at the University of Florida. Blackwood was angry, said it belonged to the hotel archives."

Santos continued making notes. "Did you notice anyone else who seemed to have issues with Blackwood?"

Mallory considered the question. "Not obvious conflicts, no. But he did mention giving us a private tour of some archive materials—items not included in his regular tours. He said, being discreet about it because, and I quote, 'Ms. Harrington prefers that certain aspects of the hotel's past remain curated for general consumption.' Those were his exact words. Kind of curious phrasing, don't you think?"

"When did he say this?" Santos asked, frowning.

"Last night, after the reception. We were planning to take his tour this morning at ten."

Santos frowned slightly. "Did he mention what specific materials he wanted to show you?"

"No, he didn't get that far," Mallory said. "But earlier, during his presentation, he'd mentioned an unsolved murder from forty years ago—a maid named Isabella Cruz who was killed in February 1985. He said she discovered something during renovations that might have led to her death."

"He discussed that during a welcome reception?" Santos asked, his eyebrows rising.

"Briefly, until Vivian cut him off," Mallory said. "She seemed uncomfortable with the topic being raised."

Santos made another note, his expression giving nothing away. "Is there anything else you can tell me about last night? Any other interactions with Blackwood that seemed significant?"

Mallory considered the question. "Not with Blackwood directly, but Judge Walter Kincaid—he's another guest—mentioned he'd been researching the Cruz murder as part of a book he's writing. He said the original police investigation was flawed."

"Judge Kincaid is here?" Santos' pen paused mid-note. "Hmm, that's interesting timing."

Before Mallory could ask what he meant by that, one of the forensic officers called Santos over to the body. The detective excused himself and conferred with his team in low voices, occasionally glancing back at Mallory.

She remained where she was, observing their procedures with interest. The crime scene team was thorough, photographing the body and surrounding area, taking samples from the tide pool, and examining the rocks nearby. One officer began methodically documenting the degraded footprints Mallory had noticed earlier.

After several minutes, Santos returned. "We'll need you to come to the station later today to make a formal statement. For now, you can return to the hotel. Please don't discuss what you've seen with the other guests. We'll be speaking with everyone individually."

"Of course," Mallory said. "Will you be treating this as a homicide investigation?"

Santos gave her a measured look. "We'll be conducting a thorough investigation into Mr. Blackwood's death. That's all I can say at this point."

Which meant yes, Mallory translated mentally. The bruising she'd seen had been obvious to her, and would certainly be evident to trained investigators.

As they made their way back up the stairs to the hotel grounds, Mallory asked, "Did Blackwood have any family?"

"No immediate family that I'm aware of," Santos replied

after a moment's hesitation. "He was something of a fixture around St. Augustine, especially in historical circles."

"How long had he worked at the Harrington?"

"Twenty years or more," Santos said. "I'd see him occasionally at the historical society meetings or the library archives. He was dedicated to his research, almost to the point of obsession."

"Research on the hotel's history?"

"Among other things," Santos allowed. "He was particularly interested in shipwrecks along the coast and salvage operations from the colonial period."

The Spanish treasure, Mallory thought, filing this confirmation away. "Did you know him well?"

"St. Augustine isn't that large," Santos replied, which wasn't really an answer. "He was a professional acquaintance only."

When they reached the hotel, they found the lobby had been transformed into an impromptu command center. Several more officers had arrived and were speaking with staff members. Tucker stood near the grand staircase, observing the proceedings with the careful attention Mallory recognized from their previous cases.

He moved to her side as soon as she entered, "You okay?" he asked quietly.

She nodded. "Fine. I just answered his questions and..." She shrugged. "And that was about it. I get the impression he knows what he's doing."

Santos rejoined his team and was immediately engaged by one of his officers, who had been questioning the night clerk.

"What did you learn?" Mallory asked Tucker in a low voice as they moved toward the parlor, away from the activity in the lobby.

"Blackwood was last seen around 10:30 PM by the night

clerk," Tucker reported. "He left through the front entrance, apparently heading toward his cottage. He often took late walks on the beach, according to the staff. Vivian is in shock. She seems genuinely distressed by his death."

"You said 'seems,'" Mallory said. "You're not convinced?"

Tucker shrugged. "She's definitely upset, but there's something else there. When I mentioned that you'd found evidence suggesting murder rather than an accident, she had an interesting reaction. Said something like, 'I was afraid of this,' before catching herself."

"She said 'Not again' when I told her," Mallory said. "Detective Santos reacted when I mentioned Judge Kincaid, too. He said it was 'interesting timing' that he's here now."

"The forty-year anniversary of Isabella Cruz's murder," Tucker mused. "February 1985 to February 2025. Significant? I wonder."

"And now another murder with possible connections to the same secrets," Mallory said. "There's no way that's coincidence."

"Maybe," Tucker said. "But we need to be careful here, Mal. This isn't our jurisdiction, and Santos didn't exactly welcome my offer to help."

"Since when has that stopped us?" Mallory asked, raising an eyebrow.

Tucker's mouth quirked in the hint of a smile. "It hasn't. But we need to be strategic. Right now, we're just hotel guests who happened to find a body. Let's keep it that way as far as Santos is concerned, while doing our own quiet investigation."

"Starting with?" Mallory asked, already knowing the answer.

"Blackwood's cottage," Tucker said. "I noticed it while you were on the beach with Santos. If he was killed because of something he knew or found, there might be evidence there. We should take a look before the police secure it."

"They haven't already?" she asked, frowning.

Tucker shook his head. "They're focused on the beach scene for now. Two officers just left to get a warrant for the cottage, but that might take some time. I heard one of the officers say the local judge is out of town."

Mallory glanced toward the lobby, where Santos was interviewing the night clerk. "How do we get to the cottage without being seen?"

"There's a side door off the parlor that leads to the gardens," Tucker said. "I saw one of the staff using it earlier. The cottage is visible from there. It's a small home with a green door, about a hundred yards into the trees."

"Well, what are we waiting for?" Mallory said, already moving toward the door. "Let's go before they finish with the clerk."

The side door opened onto a flagstone patio and a path that wound through the formal gardens before disappearing into a small wooded area. Mallory and Tucker moved quickly but casually, as if out for a morning stroll. The grounds were deserted, most of the guests apparently still in their rooms, unaware of the drama unfolding on the beach and in the lobby.

The cottage was exactly as Tucker had described; a small Victorian, brick-built house with dark green trim and a matching door nestled among live oaks draped with Spanish moss. It looked like something out of a fairy tale, picturesque against the morning light filtering through the trees.

"Quaint," Mallory commented as they approached. "Reminds me of those gingerbread houses my mom used to make at Christmas. Beautiful but potentially deadly."

Tucker tried the door, unsurprised to find it locked. "Let

me," Mallory said, already pulling her lock pick set from her pocket.

"You brought lock picks on our honeymoon?" Tucker asked, though he couldn't keep the admiration from his voice.

"I bring them everywhere," she replied, kneeling in front of the lock. "You never know when they'll come in handy." Within moments, the lock clicked open.

Mallory opened the door, and they stepped into a large living room with a small kitchen beyond. Next to the kitchen, an open door gave entry to a small bedroom with an en suite bathroom.

The living room was dominated by bookshelves over-flowing with volumes on history, archaeology, and maritime law. A desk beneath the window was piled with papers and notebooks; maps and diagrams covered one entire wall.

"Look for anything related to Isabella Cruz, the 1985 murder, or Captain Harrington's journal," Tucker instructed, already moving toward the desk. "And be careful not to disturb things more than necessary. We need to be in and out quickly."

Mallory headed for the wall of maps, scanning the diagrams for anything that might connect to their emerging puzzle. Most appeared to be historical charts of the coastline or sketches of the hotel property at various points in its development.

One diagram caught her eye: a detailed floor plan of the hotel's east wing, with certain sections highlighted in red. Handwritten notes in the margins read "1985 renovation area" and "I.C. discovery site." I.C. was for Isabella Cruz, Mallory realized. This was where the maid had been working before her murder.

"Tucker," she called softly. "Look at this."

He joined her, examining the diagram. "The east wing

renovation," he said. "Blackwood marked specific areas of interest. Look here," he pointed to a notation beside one of the highlighted sections: "Wall cavity! Possible access point?"

"Access point to what?" Mallory wondered.

"Maybe whatever Isabella Cruz found," Tucker said, taking a photo of the diagram with his phone. "Something hidden in the walls during construction that was exposed during renovations."

Meanwhile, Mallory had moved to a small table near the kitchen door where several notebooks were stacked. The top one was open to a page filled with Blackwood's meticulous handwriting. She began reading, her excitement growing as she realized what she'd found.

"Tucker, these are Blackwood's research notes on the Cruz murder," she said, scanning the page quickly. "Listen to this: 'February alignment theory confirmed by historical records. Captain's journal indicates the shadow path reveals the cache location once every 40 years when sun position matches original burial date. Next alignment: February 16, 2025.'"

"That's three days from now," Tucker said, joining her at the table.

"There's more," Mallory continued. "He continues: 'Cruz discovered something during the 1985 renovation—possibly part of the original map or a marker. V denies knowledge, but reaction suggests otherwise. Need to access east wing room 118 during alignment to confirm theory.'"

"V must be Vivian," Tucker said. "Blackwood suspected she knew more about Cruz's discovery than she admitted."

The sound of voices outside froze them both. Through the cottage window, they could see two police officers approaching along the garden path.

"Time to go," Tucker said, quickly straightening the notebook to appear undisturbed.

They slipped out through a back door and closed it behind them. Ducking behind a large stand of rhododendrons, they watched as the officers tried the front door, found it unlocked, and entered with hands on their weapons.

"That was close," Mallory whispered as they made their way through the trees, circling back toward the hotel via a different path.

"Too close," Tucker said. "But worthwhile. We now know Blackwood was researching a connection between the Cruz murder and something hidden in the hotel, something that apparently can only be located during a specific celestial alignment that happens once every forty years."

"And that alignment happens in three days," Mallory said. "Exactly forty years after Cruz was killed."

"Which means," Tucker said, "that whatever Blackwood discovered was worth killing him to keep secret. The question is, who else knows about this alignment theory? And how far are they willing to go to protect whatever is hidden in that hotel?"

As they emerged from the wooded area back onto the manicured lawn, they could see activity had increased around the hotel entrance. An ambulance had arrived, presumably to transport Blackwood's body, and more police vehicles lined the circular drive.

"We need to blend in with the other guests," Tucker said. "Act appropriately shocked and curious, but not overly interested. Let's get breakfast in the dining room and see who else is around this morning."

"And then?" Mallory asked.

"And then," he said with a tight smile, "we start investigating the past and present of the Harrington Hotel. Someone just committed murder to protect a forty-year-old secret, and I'd like to know why."

Mallory squeezed his hand as they walked toward the

hotel entrance. "So much for 'no investigations during our honeymoon,'" she teased.

"Yeah. Funny that," Tucker said. "We always seem to find trouble, don't we? Funny how it never happened before I met you. Now, here we are again, investigating a murder during what's supposed to be our romantic getaway."

"Are you kidding?" Mallory replied with a grin. "What could be more romantic than solving a decades-old mystery together? It's practically our love language."

Despite the gravity of the situation, Tucker laughed. She wasn't entirely wrong. Their relationship had been forged in the heat of investigation, their bond strengthened by the shared pursuit of truth. Now, as husband and wife, they were facing their first case together under their new titles: a honeymoon mystery that was rapidly becoming more complex and dangerous than either of them had anticipated.

4

PROFESSIONAL COURTESY

THE HARRINGTON'S DINING ROOM WAS ALREADY BUZZING WITH speculation by the time Tucker and Mallory arrived for breakfast. Word of Edwin Blackwood's death had spread quickly among the guests, though the details remained vague. Most seemed to believe it had been an unfortunate accident, a late-night fall from the bluff during one of his regular beach walks.

"Terrible tragedy," murmured a middle-aged woman at the table next to theirs as they were seated. "My husband and I were looking forward to his historical tour this morning."

"I heard he'd had too much to drink at the reception," her companion replied in a hushed voice. "Vivian should have made sure someone walked him back to his cottage."

Tucker caught Mallory's eye across their table, a silent communication passing between them. They would say nothing about the evidence of strangulation or their clandestine visit to Blackwood's cottage. For now, it was better to listen than to speak.

A server approached with coffee and menus, her eyes red-rimmed as if she'd been crying. "Good morning," she said, her voice slightly unsteady. "My name's Megan. I'll be taking care of you today."

"Thank you, Megan," Mallory said gently. "I'm sorry about Mr. Blackwood. It seems like he was well-liked by the staff."

Megan's composure faltered momentarily. "He was kind to everyone, especially the younger staff. Always had time to answer questions about the hotel's history, even silly ones from seasonal workers like me." She glanced toward the kitchen doors. "Chef Pierre is taking it especially hard. They were good friends."

Tucker filed this information away. "Pierre Dupont? The executive chef?"

"Yes, sir. They both collected historical items—artifacts and such. Used to joke about who had the better collection." Megan brushed a tear from her cheek. "Sorry, I shouldn't be bothering you with this."

"It's no bother," Mallory assured her. "Actually, we were supposed to have a kitchen tour with Chef Dupont this afternoon. I imagine that's canceled now?"

"Oh, I'm not sure," Megan replied. "The kitchen is operating, but... maybe check with the front desk later? I can take your breakfast order whenever you're ready."

They ordered quickly—eggs and toast for Tucker, Belgian waffles for Mallory—and as soon as Megan departed, Mallory leaned forward. "We need to keep that kitchen tour appointment. If Dupont and Blackwood were close, he might know what Blackwood was researching."

Tucker nodded. "Agreed. But we should talk to Detective Santos first. Establish ourselves as cooperative witnesses rather than interfering amateurs."

"Interfering professionals," Mallory corrected with a hint of a smile. "There's a difference."

"Not to local law enforcement, there isn't," Tucker

replied, though he couldn't help returning her smile. Mallory's enthusiasm was as infectious as ever. "We need to play this carefully, Mal. Build some goodwill with Santos before we start asking questions that might raise flags."

"Fine," she said. "Professional courtesy first, then our own investigation."

The dining room doors swung open, and Detective Santos entered, accompanied by a uniformed officer. The conversations around them quieted as the detective approached the hotel manager, who was speaking with an elderly couple near the buffet. After a brief exchange, Vivian nodded and gestured toward a doorway marked "Private."

"Looks like they're setting up for interviews," Tucker said. "We should finish breakfast and then offer to go next. Show our willingness to cooperate."

They ate quickly, and as they were finishing, Tucker noticed Judge Kincaid and his wife Elaine enter the dining room. The judge looked grim, while Elaine appeared alert and curious, her gaze sweeping the room as if cataloging who was present. When she spotted Tucker and Mallory, she nudged her husband and whispered something that made him glance their way.

After a moment's hesitation, the Kincaids approached their table. "Good morning," the judge said, his deep voice pitched low. "I understand you were the one who found poor Edwin?" he addressed Mallory.

"Yes," Mallory said simply, offering no details.

"Terrible business," Kincaid shook his head. "I spoke with him just last night about some historical court cases related to the hotel. He seemed in excellent spirits, eager to share his latest research findings."

"What kind of findings?" Tucker asked casually.

The judge's expression grew more guarded. "Historical minutiae, mostly. Edwin had a passion for connecting seemingly unrelated events into elaborate theories." He glanced at his wife. "We should let them finish their breakfast, my dear."

"Of course," Elaine said smoothly. "Though perhaps we could speak later? I'd be interested to hear more about your discovery this morning."

"We'll be giving our statements to Detective Santos shortly," Tucker replied. "After that, I'm sure we'll be around the hotel if you'd like to talk."

Once the Kincaids moved to their own table, Mallory raised an eyebrow. "They're awfully interested in what I saw."

"Everyone will be," Tucker replied. "That's natural curiosity. The question is why the judge seemed reluctant to discuss Blackwood's research after mentioning it himself."

They finished their breakfast and made their way to the area where Santos had set up temporary headquarters. The uniformed officer at the door informed them that the detective was currently interviewing Vivian Harrington but would be available shortly.

While they waited, Tucker watched the lobby activity. The hotel staff moved with the slightly dazed efficiency of people performing routine tasks under extraordinary circumstances. Guests clustered in small groups, exchanging theories in hushed voices. Near the front desk, Gregory Marsh stood alone, his attention focused on his phone, occasionally glancing toward the closed door behind which Santos was conducting interviews.

After about fifteen minutes, the door opened, and Vivian emerged, looking pale but composed. She nodded briefly to Tucker and Mallory before heading toward her office, her back straight, her steps measured.

"Mr. and Mrs. Randall," Santos called from the doorway. "I can take your statements now."

The room had been converted into a makeshift interview space, with a small table, several chairs, and a laptop set up for recording statements. Santos gestured for them to sit, then took his own seat across from them.

"Mrs. Randall has already given me a preliminary statement about finding the body," he said, addressing Tucker. "But I'd like to hear about your movements last night and this morning as well."

"Of course," Tucker replied. "We attended the welcome reception until about 10:15 PM, then returned to our room for the night. I woke around 6:30 this morning to find my wife had left a note saying she'd gone for a walk on the beach."

"And you didn't accompany her?" Santos asked.

"No. I was still getting ready when she returned to the room and told me about finding Blackwood's body."

Santos made a note in his notebook. "And your interactions with Mr. Blackwood last night? Did anything stand out to you?"

Tucker described the welcome reception, the historian's presentation, and the brief confrontation with Gregory Marsh. He mentioned Blackwood's offer to show them archive materials not included in the regular tour but framed it as a courtesy to honeymooning guests rather than anything suspicious.

"Did he specify what materials he wanted to show you?" Santos asked, echoing his earlier question to Mallory.

"No," Tucker said. "He just said there were items Ms. Harrington preferred to keep 'curated for general consumption.' I assumed he meant some of the more colorful aspects of the hotel's history that might not fit the upscale image they cultivate for guests."

Santos nodded, making another note. "I understand you're a former FBI agent," he said, changing directions. "And now a private investigator with your wife."

"That's correct."

"Mind if I ask what you're investigating in St. Augustine?"

"Nothing," Tucker replied honestly. "We're here on our honeymoon. We were married last week in Chattanooga."

Santos studied him for a moment. "A PI and an ex-Fed on vacation just happen to be staying at a hotel where a suspicious death occurs. That's quite a coincidence."

"It is," Tucker said calmly. "But not an impossible one. The Harrington was recommended to us by friends as a romantic getaway. We had no connection to Edwin Blackwood or any ongoing investigation in this area."

"Hmm." Santos leaned back in his chair. "And yet, your wife not only discovered the body but immediately recognized signs of foul play that wouldn't be obvious to most civilians."

"As you said, we're both investigators," Tucker pointed out. "Observing details is our job, even off-duty."

"And those details included bruising around Blackwood's neck, suggesting strangulation rather than an accidental drowning or fall," Santos stated. "Our medical examiner has completed that preliminary observation, by the way."

"I'm not surprised," Tucker said. "My wife has a good eye."

Santos considered them both for a long moment, then seemed to come to a decision. "Look, I appreciate professional courtesy, and I understand the impulse to... let's say, take an interest in cases like this, especially when you literally stumble over them. But this is my jurisdiction, and I need a clean investigation without civilian involvement, regardless of your credentials."

"We understand completely," Tucker assured him. "We're just here to enjoy our honeymoon."

Santos' expression said he didn't believe that for a second. "Right. Well, in the spirit of professional courtesy, I'll tell you what we're comfortable sharing at this point. Edwin Blackwood was murdered, likely between midnight and 2 AM based on initial estimates. He was strangled elsewhere and then placed in the tide pool, probably in hopes that the incoming tide would carry the body out to sea."

"Which would have happened if I hadn't taken that early walk," Mallory said.

"Exactly," Santos said. "The killer either didn't know the tide tables or was interrupted before they could place the body further out. Either way, it suggests some level of desperation or amateur execution."

Tucker nodded, understanding what Santos was offering —a limited information exchange to satisfy their professional curiosity while attempting to discourage further involvement. "Any leads on motive?"

"Too early to say definitively," Santos replied, which wasn't quite a refusal to share. "Blackwood had few personal enemies by all accounts, but he was also involved in several... academic disputes regarding hotel artifacts and historical research. Nothing that immediately screams motive for murder, but we're investigating all angles."

"Including the connection to Isabella Cruz's murder forty years ago?" Mallory asked directly.

A flicker of surprise crossed Santos' face before he controlled his expression. "What makes you connect those cases?"

"Blackwood mentioned Cruz during his presentation," Mallory said. "She was killed in February 1985, exactly forty years ago this month, after supposedly discovering something during hotel renovations. Now Blackwood, who was researching that cold case, turns up dead in February 2025. The timing seems significant."

Santos studied her with new interest. "You picked up a lot from a brief mention in a welcome reception."

"I pay attention," Mallory said simply.

After a moment, Santos nodded. "Yes, we're looking at

possible connections to the Cruz case, though that investigation has been cold for decades. Most of the original witnesses are deceased, and the physical evidence was... not well preserved."

"Judge Kincaid mentioned he'd been researching that case, too," Tucker offered. "He said the original investigation suffered from 'tunnel vision.'"

"Did he now?" Santos' expression hardened slightly. "Judge Kincaid has his own theories about a lot of things. I'd take them with a grain of salt if I were you."

Interesting reaction, Tucker thought. *There seems to be some history there worth exploring.*

"Was Cruz's murder ever solved?" Mallory asked, pressing the point.

"Officially, no," Santos admitted. "It remains an open but inactive case. The prevailing theory at the time was that she interrupted a burglary in progress, but no arrests were ever made." He closed his notebook decisively. "And that's all I'm comfortable sharing at this point. I appreciate your cooperation and your statements. If you remember anything else that might be relevant, please let me know."

The dismissal was clear, but Tucker agreed to make one more attempt at establishing a working relationship. "Detective, I understand your concerns about jurisdiction and interference. But given our backgrounds, if there's any way we can assist with the investigation—perhaps in an unofficial capacity—we're happy to help."

Santos considered this offer longer than Tucker expected. "I appreciate that," he said finally. "But for now, I need to conduct this investigation by the book. St. Augustine may be a small city, but we're capable of handling our own cases."

"Of course," Tucker said smoothly. "Though if you change your mind, you know where to find us."

As they rose to leave, Santos said, "One more thing—I'd

appreciate it if you'd remain available. We may have follow-up questions, and I'd prefer you not leave town until we've cleared up some basic facts."

"We're here for our honeymoon," Mallory reminded him. "We have the room booked for two weeks. We weren't planning to go anywhere."

Outside in the hallway, Mallory waited until they were well away from the interview room before murmuring, "He knows more than he's saying about the Cruz case."

"You're right," Tucker said quietly. "And he's got some history with Judge Kincaid that seems relevant. We need to find out what that's about."

"So, unofficial investigation?" Mallory asked, her eyes bright with anticipation.

"Unofficial and *discreet*," Tucker emphasized. "Santos struck me as competent but constrained—possibly by local politics or history. If we're going to learn anything useful, we need to do it without stepping on his toes or alerting potential suspects."

"Where do we start?" Mallory asked as they moved through the lobby toward the grand staircase.

"Let's split up," Tucker said. "I'll see if I can track down Francisco Ruiz, the gardener Cordelia mentioned who's related to Isabella Cruz. He might have insights that didn't make it into the official record."

"And I'll try to keep our kitchen tour with Chef Dupont," Mallory said.

Tucker nodded. "Good. We'll meet back in our room in two hours to compare notes. And Mal," he said, lowering his voice, "be careful. Remember, we're potentially dealing with someone who's already committed murder to protect whatever secret Blackwood uncovered."

"I'm always careful," she replied with a confidence that

would have worried Tucker more if he hadn't seen her handle herself in dangerous situations before.

"That's debatable," he said dryly. "Just... don't go anywhere alone with anyone, okay? Not until we have a better idea of who we can trust."

"Same goes for you," she countered. "Especially if you're talking to someone who might have information about their cousin's forty-year-old murder."

They parted in the lobby, Tucker heading for the gardens where hotel staff had indicated he might find Ruiz, while Mallory made her way toward the kitchen. As Tucker walked through the French doors onto the veranda, he spotted Gregory Marsh on his phone near the garden path, his conversation animated though his voice too low to overhear. When Marsh noticed Tucker, he quickly ended his call and pocketed his phone.

"Mr. Randall," Marsh greeted him with one of those phony professional smiles. "Quite an eventful honeymoon you're having."

"Not what we planned, that's for sure," Tucker said neutrally.

"I understand your wife found poor Edwin this morning," Marsh continued. "Terrible accident. The bluff can be treacherous in the dark."

Tucker noted Marsh's assumption—or pretense—that Blackwood's death was accidental. "The police appear to be treating it as suspicious," he replied, watching for Marsh's reaction.

A flicker of something—concern? calculation?—crossed Marsh's face before his expression smoothed into polite surprise. "Really? How bizarre. Edwin was a respected academic, if somewhat obsessive about his theories. I can't imagine who would want to harm him."

"Even after your public disagreement last night?" Tucker asked mildly.

Marsh waved a dismissive hand. "Academic squabbles are just that, academic. We disagreed about the provenance of certain historical documents, nothing worth killing over." He checked his watch. "I have a call scheduled with a client. If you'll excuse me..."

As Marsh walked away, Tucker considered his reaction. The antiques dealer had seemed genuinely surprised that Blackwood's death was being treated as suspicious, but there was something calculated in his response, as if he was choosing his words carefully.

Tucker continued along the garden path, mentally cataloging what they knew so far: *Edwin Blackwood had been researching a connection between Isabella Cruz's 1985 murder and some secret hidden within the hotel, possibly related to the rumored Spanish treasure. He'd discovered evidence of a celestial alignment occurring once every forty years that supposedly revealed the location of whatever was hidden. That alignment would occur in three days, on February 16th. And what was that about Room 118?*

Someone killed Blackwood to prevent him from following that alignment to its conclusion. The question is, who else knew about his discovery? And would they kill again to keep the secret buried?

5

PAPER TRAILS

WHILE TUCKER HEADED TO THE GARDENS IN SEARCH OF Francisco Ruiz, Mallory made her way toward the hotel's kitchen. The dining room was emptying as breakfast service ended, and the wait staff moved efficiently between tables, clearing dishes and resetting for lunch.

Mallory approached one of the servers and said with a friendly smile, "Excuse me, I had arranged a kitchen tour with Chef Dupont this afternoon. Given the circumstances with Mr. Blackwood, I wanted to check to see if it's still on."

The server hesitated. "Chef is... quite upset about Mr. Blackwood. They were close friends. But I can ask if you'd like."

"I'd appreciate that," Mallory replied. "Maybe mention that I'm interested in historical cooking methods and Mr. Blackwood had suggested I should speak with Chef Dupont about his antique cookbook collection."

While the server nodded and disappeared through the swinging kitchen doors, Mallory took the opportunity to observe the dining room more carefully. At a corner table, Elaine Kincaid sat alone, apparently waiting for her husband to return. She was writing something in a small leather-bound notebook, her attention focused and expression intense. When she sensed Mallory's gaze, she looked up, closed the notebook abruptly, and offered a tight smile.

Before Mallory could decide whether to approach her, the server returned. "Chef says he can see you now, but only briefly. He has meal preparations to oversee."

"Thank you," Mallory said, following the server through the swinging doors into the kitchen's controlled chaos.

The Harrington's kitchen was a blend of historic charm and modern efficiency. Copper pots hung from ceiling racks, and a massive antique stove stood along one wall, seemingly more for decoration than practical use. The working areas featured gleaming stainless steel and the latest equipment.

In the center of this domain stood Chef Pierre Dupont, a stocky man in his mid-forties with thinning dark hair and the intense expression of someone who demands perfection. He was issuing rapid-fire instructions to his staff, but paused when he noticed Mallory.

"Mrs. Randall," he said, his French accent more pronounced than it had been during their brief conversation at the reception. "You wished to see me?"

"Yes, thank you for making time," Mallory said. "I know this must be a difficult day. I understand you and Mr. Blackwood were friends."

A shadow crossed Dupont's face. "Edwin was a good man, a true scholar." He glanced around at his busy staff, then gestured toward a small office at the back of the kitchen. "Come. We can speak privately for a few minutes."

The office was barely large enough for a desk and two chairs, with shelves above crowded with cookbooks. Many appeared to be antique volumes with faded leather bindings. A framed photograph on the desk showed a younger Dupont and Blackwood, arms around each other's shoulders, standing in front of what looked like ancient ruins.

"Please, sit," Dupont said, gesturing to the chair across from his desk while he settled into his own with a heavy sigh. "What did you wish to discuss? You mentioned historical cooking methods?"

"Yes," Mallory began, deciding on a direct approach. "But honestly, I'm more interested in your friendship with Edwin Blackwood. I'm so sorry about what happened to him."

Dupont's expression darkened. "It was no accident. Edwin would never have fallen. He knew those cliffs like his own reflection."

"I agree," Mallory said carefully. "When I found him this morning, there were signs suggesting his death wasn't an accident."

Dupont's eyes widened slightly, but he didn't seem shocked by the revelation. "The police, they are treating it as murder?"

"A suspicious death, yes. Detective Santos confirmed it."

The chef nodded slowly, as if this confirmed his suspicions. "Edwin feared something like this might happen. He said he was getting too close."

"Too close to what?" Mallory asked, leaning forward.

Dupont hesitated, studying her. "Why do you ask these questions, Mrs. Randall? You are a guest on honeymoon, no?"

"My husband and I are private investigators," Mallory admitted. "We're here on our honeymoon, but given what's happened... we can't help being curious."

"Ah." Dupont considered this, then seemed to make a decision. "Edwin was my friend for many years. We shared a passion for history, for artifacts." He gestured to the shelves of old cookbooks. "I collect these—historical recipes, cooking methods from colonial times. Edwin collected... broader items. Maritime history, primarily."

"Related to the Spanish treasure fleet?" Mallory asked.

Dupont's eyebrows rose. "He mentioned this to you?"

"During his presentation last night," she replied. "Before Vivian cut him off."

A bitter smile crossed the chef's face. "Yes, Vivian prefers that certain aspects of the hotel's history remain... shall we say, sanitized? But the treasure is real, Mrs. Randall. Or was. Edwin believed he had finally found proof of where Captain Harrington hid his acquisitions from the 1715 fleet."

"And where was that?" she asked.

"Somewhere within the hotel itself," Dupont replied, lowering his voice despite the office door being closed. "Hidden during the original construction, accessible only through architectural features that align during a specific celestial event."

"The February alignment," Mallory said, testing whether Dupont knew this detail.

The chef nodded, not surprised she knew. "Yes. Every forty years, the sun's position reveals the location through shadow patterns across the property. Edwin discovered some old diagrams in Captain Harrington's papers suggesting this method was intentional—a way to ensure only family members who knew the secret could access the cache."

"And this alignment happens soon?" she asked.

"February 16th," Dupont said. "Three days from now. Edwin was certain this was why Isabella Cruz was killed forty years ago. She discovered something during the renovations—possibly part of the mechanism or a marker—that revealed the secret. And now..." his voice trailed off, emotion overwhelming him momentarily.

"Now Edwin has been killed," Mallory finished quietly.

Dupont nodded, composing himself. "Three nights ago, Edwin came to me, very excited. He had found something in the east wing—Room 118. A small compartment behind a wall panel that contained papers. Old documents he believed were part of the original map to the treasure's location. He planned to return during the alignment to confirm his theory."

"Did he tell anyone else about this discovery?"

"He intended to tell Vivian," Dupont said, his expression troubled. "Though they had their disagreements, he believed the Harrington family had the right to know first. But he wanted to confirm his theory before he approached her."

"Did he mention anyone else who might have known about his discovery? Gregory Marsh? Judge Kincaid? Cordelia Winters?"

Dupont's eyes narrowed at the mention of Marsh. "Marsh has been trying to acquire the Harrington artifacts for years. He represents a wealthy collector who is obsessed with the 1715 fleet. Edwin caught him once in the archives without permission, photographing documents."

"And the others?" she pressed.

"The judge... Edwin mentioned he had been asking unusually specific questions about the east wing renovations from 1985. As for Ms. Winters—" Dupont was interrupted by a knock at the office door.

One of the kitchen staff poked her head in. "Chef, the lunch preparations..."

"Oui, j'arrive," Dupont replied, then turned back to Mallory. "I must return to work. But there is something you should know. Edwin kept a second set of research notes—his most important discoveries—in a safe deposit box at the Coastal Bank on King Street. He gave me a letter to be opened in the event of his death." Dupont reached into his desk drawer and removed a sealed envelope. "Perhaps it contains access information."

Mallory accepted the envelope, surprised by this development. "Thank you for trusting me with this."

Dupont stood, his expression grave. "I trust you because Edwin's death was no accident, and the local police... they have their limitations. Politics in St. Augustine runs deep, especially where the Harrington Hotel is concerned." He glanced at his watch. "You should go now. But be careful, Mrs. Randall, because whatever Edwin discovered was worth killing for once, so it could be again, no?"

MEANWHILE, Tucker's search for Francisco Ruiz had led him to the far corner of the hotel grounds, where the manicured gardens gave way to a more natural landscape. A small tool shed stood beneath the spreading branches of a massive live oak draped with Spanish moss.

As Tucker approached, he saw an elderly man on his knees, carefully tending to a bed of native plants. Despite his age—he had to be in his mid-seventies, at least—his weathered hands moved with certainty among the greenery.

"Mr. Ruiz?" Tucker called, not wanting to startle the man.

The gardener looked up, his dark eyes narrowed, assessing Tucker from beneath bushy white eyebrows. "Sí?"

"My name is Tucker Randall. I'm staying at the hotel. I was hoping I might speak with you for a few minutes."

Ruiz slowly rose to his feet, wincing slightly as his knees straightened. "About the gardens? I give tours on Thursdays."

"Actually, it's about Edwin Blackwood," Tucker said. "And about your cousin, Isabella Cruz."

The gardener went very still, his expression closing off. "I have work to do," he said, turning back to his plants.

"I understand your reluctance," Tucker said calmly. "But my wife found Mr. Blackwood's body this morning. We believe he was murdered, and we think it might be connected to what happened to your cousin forty years ago."

Ruiz's hands stilled in the soil. After a long moment, he sighed and straightened again. "Why do you care about things that happened so long ago? You are a guest, no? Here on vacation?"

"My wife and I are private investigators," Tucker explained. "And while we are here on our honeymoon, we can't ignore what's happened. Especially if there's a connection to an older case."

Ruiz studied him carefully, then gestured toward a small bench beneath the oak tree. "Sit. My old knees can't stand too long these days."

Tucker joined him on the bench, noticing how the gardener positioned himself to keep the tool shed in view, as if concerned about being seen.

"Isabella was like a daughter to me," Ruiz began, his voice low. "Her parents died when she was young, and my wife and I helped raise her. She was a good girl—hardworking, honest. When she got the job here at the Harrington, we were proud. Good pay, prestigious place." His expression darkened. "Then they started the renovations in the east wing."

"The 1985 renovations," Tucker asked.

Ruiz nodded. "Isabella was assigned to clean up after the workers each day. One evening, she came to our house, very excited but also frightened. She had found something in the walls; something valuable, she said. Papers and a small golden object with strange markings. She didn't know what to do, whether to report it or…"

"Or keep it?" Tucker said when Ruiz trailed off.

The old man shrugged. "She was young, poor. The temptation was strong. I told her to return it, that keeping it would be theft. She agreed to speak with Ms. Harrington the next day." His eyes grew distant with memory. "That was the last time I saw her alive."

"What happened?"

"They found her body near the beach stairs, not far from where your wife found Edwin this morning. Police said she was attacked, robbed. But nothing was taken—her purse, her jewelry, all still there. And whatever she had found... that disappeared."

"Did you tell the police about what she'd discovered in the walls?"

Ruiz's laugh was bitter. "Of course. They didn't believe me. Said I was making up stories to explain a simple robbery gone wrong. The detective in charge... he was close with the Harrington family. The case was closed quickly."

"And the Harringtons? What was their response?"

"Old Mr. Harrington—Vivian's father—he offered condolences, paid for the funeral. Vivian was younger then, and recently returned from college to help manage the hotel. She seemed genuinely upset about Isabella's death."

"But?" Tucker sensed there was more.

Ruiz hesitated, then lowered his voice further. "Two weeks after Isabella died, I saw workmen late at night, removing something from the east wing; heavy objects, wrapped carefully. They loaded them into a van with no markings. When I asked about it the next day, I was told it was just construction debris. But construction debris, they don't wrap it so carefully, no?"

"Did you ever mention this to anyone?" Tucker asked.

"To the police, yes. Again, they dismissed it. They said renovations always produce unusual activities." Ruiz looked down at his soil-stained hands. "After that, I kept quiet. I had a family to support. I needed my job here. But I watched and listened. For forty years, I have watched and listened."

"And what have you learned in that time?" Tucker asked.

Ruiz's eyes met his. They were sharp with age and wisdom. "That the Harrington family protects its own. And that Edwin Blackwood was getting too close to the truth." He glanced toward the hotel, his expression troubled. "Last week, he showed me an old diagram—architectural plans for the east wing—and he asked me if I remembered a particular wall section that had been renovated in 1985. The same area where Isabella had been working."

"And did you?" Tucker pressed.

"Sí. Room 118 is now a small library for guests. Before the renovation, it was a storage room, rarely used. Edwin believed something was hidden there, something revealed only during a specific alignment of sun and shadow that occurs every forty years."

"On February 16th," Tucker said.

Ruiz nodded, unsurprised that Tucker knew this detail. "Sí. Three days from now. The same date Isabella died forty years ago." He leaned closer. "Edwin found something in that room, behind the new paneling. Papers, he said. He was very excited but also nervous. Said he needed to study them carefully before deciding what to do."

"Did he say what the papers contained?" Tucker asked.

"No, but he asked me about the old Harrington cemetery on the property. It's mostly forgotten now. The family started using the city cemetery in the 1920s. But there's a small plot near the edge of the grounds, overgrown, abandoned. Edwin thought it was significant somehow."

Tucker filed this information away. "Mr. Ruiz, who do you think killed your cousin? And Edwin Blackwood?"

The old gardener was silent for a long moment, seemingly weighing how much to share. Finally, he said, "I cannot accuse without proof. But the Harrington treasure—if it exists—would be worth millions today. People have killed for much less." He stood slowly. "I must return to work now. Ms. Harrington does not like to see me idle."

"One more question," Tucker said, rising as well. "Do you know Detective Santos? He's investigating Blackwood's murder."

A flicker of recognition crossed Ruiz's face. "Diego Santos. Yes, I know of him. His mother, Gloria Mendez, she works here. She is head housekeeper. She was friends with Isabella." Ruiz's expression grew guarded. "Be careful what you say to him. His mother has worked for the Harringtons for over forty years. Her loyalty is... complicated."

"Understood," Tucker said. "Thank you for speaking with me, Mr. Ruiz."

As the gardener walked away, returning to his plants, Tucker considered what he'd learned. The connection between the two murders seemed increasingly clear: both victims had discovered something related to the hidden Harrington treasure. *Motive enough, I suppose,* he thought.

But who had killed them to protect that secret? The Harrington family had the most obvious motive: to preserve their legacy and whatever wealth might be hidden on the property. But others: Gregory Marsh with his wealthy client, Judge Kincaid with his suspiciously specific research interests, even Cordelia Winters with her literary ambitions, they all had potential motives as well.

Tucker checked his watch. It was nearly time to meet Mallory back in their room to compare notes. As he walked back toward the hotel, he spotted Gloria Mendez—recognizable from Ruiz's description as the elderly Hispanic woman who had left the reception when Blackwood mentioned Isabella Cruz—directing a team of housekeepers near the main entrance.

Their eyes met briefly, and Tucker nodded politely. She returned the gesture, her expression carefully neutral, before turning back to her staff. But something in her gaze—a flicker of assessment, perhaps even recognition—said she knew exactly who he was and why he'd been speaking with Francisco Ruiz.

It seemed everyone was watching everyone else, guarding secrets that had festered for forty years. The question was whether those secrets were worth killing for—again.

———————————

BACK IN THEIR SUITE, Tucker arrived to find Mallory already there, pacing excitedly. She turned at the sound of the door, her eyes bright with the familiar enthusiasm of a promising lead.

"You found something," Tucker said.

"A lot of somethings," she said, holding up a sealed envelope. "Blackwood left this with Chef Dupont, to be opened in the event of his death. It might contain access information for a safe deposit box where Blackwood kept his most important research findings."

Tucker raised his eyebrows, impressed. "That's a significant break. Anything else?"

"Dupont said that Blackwood had found something in Room 118 in the east wing—documents hidden behind a wall panel he believed were related to the treasure's location. He was planning to wait until the February 16th alignment to confirm his theory." Mallory sat on the edge of the bed. "How about you? Any luck with Ruiz?"

Tucker nodded, moving to sit beside her. "He was surprisingly forthcoming once I mentioned Isabella Cruz. Said much of what we already suspected, that his cousin found something during the 1985 renovations in the same Room 118, something valuable enough to get her killed."

"The east wing again," Mallory said. "And Room 118 specifically."

"Ruiz also mentioned something interesting," he continued. "An old Harrington family cemetery on the property that's been abandoned since the 1920s. Blackwood had been asking questions about it. He thought it might be significant somehow."

"Connected to the treasure location, maybe?" Mallory said. "Or perhaps where something was hidden?"

"Possibly," Tucker said. "Ruiz also told me that Detective Santos' mother is Gloria Mendez, the head housekeeper who's worked here for over forty years. She was friends with Isabella Cruz back in 1985."

Mallory's eyes widened. "That's a significant connection. Do you think Santos is involved in the cover-up?"

"I don't know," Tucker said thoughtfully. "Ruiz warned me to be careful what I say to him, suggesting Gloria's loyalty to the Harrington family might complicate things. But Santos seems like a competent detective. He could simply be trying to conduct a clean investigation without letting family connections interfere."

"Or he could be deliberately steering the investigation away from certain avenues, just like the detective forty years ago," Mallory countered. "We should be careful what we share with him."

Tucker nodded in agreement. "For now, let's focus on what we know and what we need to find out next. We have three days until this alignment that supposedly reveals the treasure's location. In the meantime, we need to figure out who killed Blackwood and why."

"And access that safe deposit box," Mallory said, turning the envelope over in her hands. "Should we open it now?"

Tucker hesitated, considering the legal implications. "Technically, we're not the intended recipients of whatever's in there. But if it contains information relevant to Blackwood's murder..."

"Which it almost certainly does," Mallory pointed out. "He didn't address it to anyone, and he left specific instructions for it to be opened if something happened to him."

"Alright," Tucker said. "Let's see what Blackwood wanted found after his death."

Mallory carefully opened the envelope and removed a single folded sheet of paper. As she unfolded it, a small key fell onto the bedspread, the kind used for safe deposit boxes. The paper contained a brief handwritten note:

"To whomever opens this in the event of my demise:

The key enclosed provides access to safe deposit box #247 at Coastal Bank on King Street. The box contains my most significant research findings regarding the Harrington Hotel and its secrets, including documentation of the February alignment theory and evidence connecting Isabella Cruz's murder to these discoveries. The box is registered under the name 'James Carpenter' (my maternal grandfather's name) with my birth date as the secondary identification.

If you are reading this, I likely met an untimely end related to these discoveries. Do not trust obvious appearances. The Harrington treasure is real, but its true nature is not what most believe. The answer lies not in gold or artifacts but in legacy and blood.

Edwin Blackwood"

"Legacy and blood," Mallory repeated softly. "What do you think that means?"

Tucker frowned, considering the cryptic message. "Could be metaphorical, referring to the Harrington family bloodline. Or literal—someone killed for this secret."

"Or both," Mallory said. "Ruiz mentioned Blackwood was interested in the old family cemetery. Blood and legacy could refer to family secrets buried there, literally and figuratively."

Tucker nodded, impressed as always by Mallory's intuitive leaps. "We need to access that safe deposit box. Banks are closed on Sundays, so we'll have to wait until tomorrow."

"What about Room 118 in the east wing?" Mallory asked. "Shouldn't we check that out too? See if we can find where Blackwood discovered those documents?"

"It's risky," Tucker cautioned. "If it's a guest library, as Ruiz mentioned, there could be people there. Plus, if Santos has connected the dots like we have, he might have that room under surveillance."

"We'll need to be careful, then," Mallory said. "Maybe do a casual reconnaissance first, see the layout, determine when it's least likely to be occupied."

Tucker checked his watch. "It's almost noon. Why don't we take a walk through the hotel, locate Room 118, and see what we're dealing with? Play the part of curious honeymooners exploring the historic property."

"Perfect," Mallory said, standing and smoothing her shirt. "And afterward, maybe we should find Judge Kincaid. Blackwood's note warned not to trust obvious appearances, and the judge seems very interested in the same historical events we're investigating."

"Good thinking," Tucker said, pocketing the key. "But we need to be careful about how much we reveal. Everyone here has an agenda, and until we know more about who killed Blackwood, we can't trust anyone."

"Except each other," Mallory reminded him with a smile.

Tucker returned the smile, reaching for her hand. "That goes without saying."

As they prepared to leave their room, Tucker couldn't help reflecting on the irony of their situation. They'd come to St. Augustine seeking a peaceful honeymoon and instead found themselves embroiled in a deadly mystery spanning forty years. Yet he couldn't deny that part of him relished the challenge—the intellectual puzzle, the careful gathering of evidence, the collaboration with Mallory that had always been the foundation of both their professional and personal relationships.

This wasn't the honeymoon they'd planned, but in some ways, it was perfectly them: even when it meant placing themselves in danger. And the question was whether they could solve this mystery before the killer struck again, and if the February alignment in three days time would reveal anything… anything worth killing for.

And if the past was any indication, the answer was likely yes.

6

HIDDEN CONNECTIONS

Tucker and Mallory set out from their room, ostensibly as nothing more than curious honeymooners exploring their historic accommodations. They wandered the grand hallways hand in hand, pausing occasionally to admire architectural details or vintage photographs while gradually making their way toward the east wing.

"According to the floor map by the elevator, room 118 is on the second floor," Mallory murmured, leaning close as if sharing a romantic observation.

They descended the grand staircase to the lobby, where police activity had diminished but not disappeared entirely. Two uniformed officers stood near the front desk, speaking with Vivian Harrington, whose composure appeared to be strained by the ongoing intrusion into her carefully ordered establishment.

"Let's take the long way around," Tucker said quietly. "Through the parlor and that side hallway we saw earlier."

They strolled casually through the parlor, now set up for afternoon tea with delicate china and silver services. Guests sat in small clusters, their conversations hushed but animated; no doubt discussing the morning's grim discovery.

In the side hallway, they encountered Gloria Mendez—a large, older woman with silver hair tied up in a bun—directing a young housekeeper. The older woman's eyes narrowed slightly as she noticed Tucker and Mallory approach.

"Good afternoon," Tucker greeted her politely. "We're exploring the historic sections of the hotel. I understand the east wing has some particularly interesting architecture?"

Gloria's expression remained neutral, but her eyes were watchful. "Yes, sir. The east wing contains the original library and some of the hotel's oldest guest rooms. The staircase at the end of this hall will take you there."

"Thank you," Mallory said with a bright smile. "It's such a beautiful property. You must have seen many changes over the years you've worked here."

Something flickered across Gloria's face. Was it caution, perhaps, or calculation? Mallory wondered. "Some things change. Others remain the same." She turned to the young housekeeper. "Maria, please finish the Magnolia Suite next."

As the housekeeper moved away, Gloria said in a lower voice, "The east wing library closes for cleaning at three o'clock. It's usually empty then." Then, without waiting for a response, she turned away and continued down the hallway, her back straight, her steps purposeful.

Tucker and Mallory exchanged a meaningful glance as they reached the staircase Gloria had indicated.

"Was that a hint?" Mallory whispered as they climbed the stairs.

"I think it was," Tucker replied quietly. "But whether it's meant to help or hinder us remains to be seen."

The east wing corridor was narrower than the main halls, with lower ceilings and darker woodwork, architecture of a bygone era. Brass sconces provided soft lighting that enhanced the historic atmosphere. Numbered doors lined both sides of the hallway.

They moved slowly, noting room numbers as they passed. 110... 112... 114... Around a slight bend in the corridor, they found Room 118, its door bearing a small brass plaque with the words "Harrington Library" thereon.

Tucker tried the handle. The door was unlocked. The room beyond was small but elegant, with floor-to-ceiling bookshelves on three walls and a large window overlooking the gardens on the fourth. A central table surrounded by four chairs occupied most of the floor space, while two wingback chairs flanked a small catacorner fireplace to the right of the window. The room was empty of people.

"Perfect. What a lovely room," Mallory murmured, moving to examine the bookshelves while Tucker positioned himself near the door, able to observe the hallway through the small window in the door's upper panel.

"What exactly are we looking for?" Mallory asked quietly, running her fingers along the ornate wood paneling between bookshelves.

"According to what Dupont told you, Blackwood found documents behind a wall panel," Tucker replied. "Look for any section that might be removable or seem newer than the rest."

Mallory methodically examined each section of paneled wall on either side of the window, tapping gently here and there, feeling for inconsistencies in the wood. Meanwhile, Tucker kept watch and began scanning the book titles, noting that most related to Florida history, maritime law, or the Spanish colonial period.

"Tucker," Mallory called softly, "I think I found something."

He joined her at the far corner of the room to the left of

the fireplace, where she was examining a section of paneling beside the fireplace. The woodwork appeared identical to the surrounding walls, but when Mallory pressed a particular spot, a small section moved slightly.

"There's definitely something here," she murmured, carefully working her fingers along the edge until she found a nearly invisible catch. With a soft click, a panel approximately two feet square swung inward, revealing a small cavity behind.

"Empty," Tucker said, shining his phone's flashlight into the space. "Blackwood must have removed whatever was hidden here."

"Not quite empty," Mallory countered, reaching in carefully. Her fingers emerged with a small scrap of paper that had apparently fallen into a crack at the bottom of the cavity. "Look at this."

The scrap contained a partial drawing that appeared to be a segment of a map with a distinctive compass rose in one corner. The edges were torn, suggesting it had been separated from a larger document, perhaps accidentally, when Blackwood removed the rest of the contents.

"Part of the map Blackwood found," Tucker surmised, examining the fragment. "Not much to go on, but it confirms he did find something here."

A sound from the hallway alerted them. Tucker quickly closed the hidden panel while Mallory pocketed the map fragment. They had just seated themselves at the central table, pretending to examine a book on maritime history, when the door opened.

Judge Kincaid stood in the doorway, his bushy eyebrows rising in surprise. "Mr. and Mrs. Randall. I didn't expect to find anyone here."

The judge, an older man in his late sixties, tall, austere, with a full head of gray hair swept back into what in a younger man might have been called a mullet, looked more than a little perturbed to find them there.

"Judge," Tucker acknowledged calmly. "We were exploring the historic portions of the hotel. This is a beautiful room."

"Indeed it is," Kincaid said, entering and closing the door behind him. His gaze swept the room with particular attention to the paneled walls. "One of my favorites in the hotel. So much history in these walls."

The emphasis he placed on the last words was subtle, but unmistakable. Tucker exchanged a quick glance with Mallory, confirming she'd noticed it too.

"We were just reading about the Spanish treasure fleet," Mallory said, gesturing to the open book on the table. "Fascinating history."

"Very," Kincaid said, moving to the bookshelf nearest the fireplace—precisely where the hidden panel was located. "The 1715 fleet, in particular, has captured imaginations for centuries. Eleven ships lost in a hurricane, carrying wealth beyond imagining... and Captain Harrington was one of the few to successfully salvage significant portions."

"You seem quite knowledgeable about it," Tucker said, looking up at him.

"It intersects with several legal cases I've studied," Kincaid explained, running his hand along the bookshelf in a seemingly casual gesture. "Maritime salvage law was effectively shaped by recovery efforts from that fleet."

"Mr. Blackwood mentioned something about that in his presentation," Mallory said, watching the judge's movements carefully. "Before he was... interrupted."

Kincaid's hand paused momentarily. "Yes, poor Edwin. Quite a loss to the historical community. We had several stimulating discussions about the Harrington family's connection to the 1715 fleet." His fingers continued their subtle exploration of the paneling. "He had some particularly interesting theories about artifacts hidden on the property."

"Is that what you're researching for your book?" Tucker asked.

Kincaid turned, studying them both with new intensity. "Among other things, yes. Historical legal precedents relating to salvage rights primarily, but the human elements make for a more compelling narrative." His expression grew somber. "Including how far people might go to protect valuable secrets."

"Like murder?" Mallory said boldly.

The judge's bushy gray eyebrows rose, but he didn't appear shocked by her directness. "An unfortunate but not uncommon outcome when substantial wealth is involved. Both forty years ago and, perhaps, today."

"You're referring to Isabella Cruz," Tucker said.

"And Edwin Blackwood," Kincaid said. "Two deaths, forty years apart, both connected to the same mystery." He moved away from the wall, seating himself in one of the wingback chairs. "I understand you're private investigators. Not just honeymooners, after all."

"Word travels fast," Tucker said.

"It's a small hotel," Kincaid replied with a thin smile. "And in my experience, coincidences rarely exist. Your presence here, with your particular skills, at this specific moment... interesting timing."

"We could say the same about you," Mallory countered. "A retired judge researching historical legal cases connected to the hotel's past, staying here during the exact anniversary of an unsolved murder."

Kincaid chuckled, apparently appreciating her directness. "Fair point, Mrs. Randall. Let me be frank; I've been researching the Harrington case for years. It's the center-piece of my book on how wealthy families have used legal maneuvering to protect questionable assets throughout American history."

"And what have you discovered?" Tucker asked.

"That the Harrington treasure isn't quite what people imagine," Kincaid replied. "Yes, there are likely valuable artifacts hidden somewhere on the property. But the real secret —what people have died to protect—is the documentation proving their provenance."

"Why would provenance documentation be worth killing over?" Mallory asked, leaning forward with interest.

"Because," Kincaid said, lowering his voice, "if my research is correct, Captain Harrington obtained those artifacts through means that were questionable even by 19th-century standards. Methods that would invalidate the family's claim and potentially open them to significant liability today."

Before he could elaborate, the door opened again. Elaine Kincaid stood in the doorway, her expression shifting from surprise to careful neutrality when she saw her husband wasn't alone.

"Walter, there you are, darling," she said smoothly, a slightly sardonic smile on her startlingly red lips. "I've been looking everywhere for you. The front desk has that call you were expecting."

"Ah, my publisher," Kincaid explained, rising. "You'll have to excuse me." He paused at the door. "Perhaps we can continue our discussion later. I believe we share some... common interests."

After the Kincaids departed, Tucker and Mallory remained silent for a moment, processing what they'd learned.

"She's got to be half his age," Mallory muttered.

"A trophy wife, I think," Tucker said, nodding thoughtfully.

"He was looking for the hidden compartment, wasn't he?" Mallory said.

"I think he was," Tucker said. "And I also think he knows more than he's sharing. The question is, is he investigating or is he somehow involved?"

"And what did he mean about questionable means of obtaining the artifacts?" Mallory wondered. "Theft? Fraud?"

"Whatever it is, it connects to the February alignment in three days," Tucker said, checking his watch. "It's nearly three o'clock. Gloria mentioned the library would be closed for cleaning. We should go."

They left Room 118, carefully closing the door behind them. As they walked back toward the main staircase, Tucker couldn't shake the feeling that they were being watched. The Harrington Hotel was full of eyes, some curious, some calculating, and at least one pair that belonged to a killer.

7

THE SECOND BODY

THE REST OF THE AFTERNOON PASSED WITHOUT INCIDENT. Tucker and Mallory spent an hour walking hand-in-hand along the beach, maintaining their honeymoon cover while discussing their findings in hushed voices amid the sound of breaking waves.

They decided to visit Coastal Bank first thing in the morning to access Blackwood's safe deposit box and planned to seek out Francisco Ruiz again for more details about the old Harrington cemetery.

By early evening, heavy clouds had begun to roll in from the Atlantic, and the temperature dropped noticeably. The hotel staff bustled about, closing beach umbrellas and securing outdoor furniture as the wind picked up. A small handwritten notice appeared in the lobby announcing that dinner would be served in the main dining room as usual, despite the approaching storm.

"Perfect weather for staying in," Mallory said as they dressed for dinner. "Though I doubt a little rain will reveal much that's been hidden for forty years."

"Maybe not," Tucker said, adjusting his tie. "But storms

have a way of changing circumstances and creating opportunities."

The dining room was about half-full when they arrived, the usual vacation atmosphere subdued by both the morning's tragedy and the worsening weather outside. Through the tall windows, they could see palm trees bending in the strengthening wind, and occasional lightning flashes illuminated the darkening beach.

Vivian Harrington stood near the entrance, greeting guests as they arrived, a commander reassuring her troops that all was well despite the dual disruptions to her carefully maintained establishment. Her smile, though still professional, appeared strained at the edges.

"Mr. and Mrs. Randall," she said as they approached. "I trust you're finding ways to enjoy your stay despite the unfortunate circumstances and now this awful weather."

"We're making the best of it," Tucker said, smiling at her. "The hotel is beautiful, even in a storm."

"Perhaps especially in a storm," Vivian replied. "The Harrington has weathered hurricanes, wars, and economic depressions for over a century. It endures." Something in her tone said she wasn't speaking only of the building.

As they were shown to their table, Tucker noticed Judge Kincaid and Elaine dining with Cordelia Winters in a corner away from the windows. Their conversation appeared intense, but was too distant to overhear.

Gregory Marsh sat alone at a small table near the windows, alternating between watching the storm outside and observing the other diners with poorly disguised interest.

"Quite the gathering of interested parties," Mallory murmured as they settled at their table. "Everyone circling each other, watching and waiting."

"For the storm to pass?" Tucker said. "Or for the alignment in three days?"

"Both, maybe," Mallory replied, opening her menu. "The storm gives everyone a perfect excuse to stay inside, keep an eye on each other... and on Room 118."

Their server Megan, who had attended them at breakfast. "Good evening. The chef's special tonight is Gulf shrimp with saffron risotto. We also have a lovely duck breast with cherry reduction."

They placed their orders, and as Megan turned to leave, the lights flickered momentarily. A murmur ran through the dining room.

"It's just the storm," Vivian announced from near the entrance, her voice carrying with practiced authority. "Our generators will activate automatically if necessary. Please continue your meals without concern."

As if to challenge her assurance, a particularly bright flash of lightning was followed almost immediately by a tremendous crack of thunder. The lights flickered again and then went out completely, plunging the dining room into darkness, broken only by the candles on each table and occasional lightning flashes through the windows.

For a moment, there was silence, then a rising murmur of voices; some concerned, others amused by the atmospheric interruption to their meal. The staff moved in quickly, bringing additional candles to each table.

"Ladies and gentlemen," Vivian's voice cut through the darkness. "Please remain seated. Our emergency generators should activate momentarily. This is a common occurrence during coastal storms and nothing to be concerned about."

Tucker felt rather than saw Mallory lean closer across the table. "Perfect opportunity for someone to slip away unnoticed," she whispered.

He nodded, though she probably couldn't see the gesture clearly. "Try to keep track of our key players," he whispered.

In the dim candlelight, Tucker could just make out the shapes of other diners. Judge Kincaid and his companions remained at their table, their silhouettes visible against the window when lightning flashed. Gregory Marsh's table, however, was empty.

The emergency lights came on a few minutes later; not full illumination, but enough light to navigate the room safely. Vivian checked on several tables, her composure never wavering despite the disruption.

"As you can see, the generators are running," she announced. "We'll have partial power throughout the hotel until the main electricity is restored. Chef Dupont assures me that dinner service will continue without interruption."

As if on cue, servers began emerging from the kitchen with appetizers and drinks. The natural human relief at the return of light, combined with the dramatic backdrop of the storm, seemed to elevate the mood in the dining room, and conversation returned to normal.

"Marsh is gone," Mallory said quietly. "He must have slipped out during the blackout."

"Could just be stepping out to make a call or use the restroom," Tucker replied, though his instincts said otherwise.

Their appetizers arrived, and they ate while maintaining their casual surveillance of the room. Gregory Marsh returned about ten minutes later, sliding back into his seat with a quick glance around to see if his absence had been noticed. Nothing in his demeanor said anything out of the ordinary, but Tucker made a mental note of the timing.

The rest of their meal passed uneventfully, the storm continuing to rage outside while the hotel operated on generator power. As they finished dessert, their server approached again.

"Chef Dupont would like to know if everything was satisfactory," Megan said, her expression suggesting this was not a routine inquiry.

"Everything was excellent," Mallory replied. "Please convey our compliments to the chef."

"He'd like to hear them personally, if you have a moment," Megan continued, lowering her voice. "He asked if you might stop by the kitchen before returning to your room."

Tucker and Mallory exchanged a glance. "Of course," Tucker said. "We'd be happy to."

After signing their check, they made their way toward the kitchen, passing through the now half-empty dining room. The storm showed no signs of abating. The rain lashed against the windows in horizontal sheets driven by the powerful wind.

The kitchen was illuminated by emergency lighting, creating dramatic shadows among the stainless steel work-stations. Several staff members were cleaning up, but there was no sign of Chef Dupont.

"Chef asked to see us," Mallory explained to a sous chef, who approached them with a questioning look.

"He should be in the walk-in," the young man replied, gesturing toward a heavy metal door at the back of the kitchen. "Doing inventory during the power outage to make sure nothing spoils."

They crossed the kitchen, aware of curious glances from the staff. The walk-in freezer door was slightly ajar, a strip of light visible around its edges.

"Chef Dupont?" Tucker called, pushing the door open wider.

The freezer was large; a small room with shelves of food along both sides and hanging hooks for meat at the far end.

The emergency lighting cast an eerie bluish glow over the interior. And on the floor, partially obscured by a fallen shelf of frozen seafood, lay Chef Pierre Dupont, his eyes open and fixed, a thin line of frost already forming on his eyebrows and lashes.

Mallory gasped softly. Tucker immediately pulled her back, partially closing the door behind him.

"Get Detective Santos," he instructed a startled kitchen worker who had approached behind them. "Tell him there's been another death."

The next hour passed slowly. Police officers and medical personnel arrived in force, working by emergency lighting to process the scene. Guests were asked to remain in the public areas of the hotel while statements were taken. Detective Santos, looking grim and increasingly suspicious, interviewed Tucker and Mallory separately about why they had gone to the kitchen after dinner.

"Chef Dupont asked to see us," Mallory explained, for the third time. "He sent our server, Megan, with the message."

"And what did you assume this meeting was about?" Santos pressed.

"I thought perhaps he wanted to reschedule our kitchen tour," Mallory replied, which was technically true, if incomplete. "It was supposed to happen this afternoon but never did, given the circumstances with Mr. Blackwood."

Santos studied her face for a long moment. "Two deaths in one day, Mrs. Randall. Both discovered by or connected to you and your husband. That's quite the coincidence."

"We were as surprised as anyone," Mallory replied, quietly. "Is it definitely murder?"

Santos' expression revealed nothing. "The medical examiner will make that determination. But the freezer door cannot be locked from the inside, and Chef Dupont knew that facility better than anyone. It's unlikely he would accidentally trap himself inside."

"The power outage would have been the perfect opportunity," Mallory said. "Confusion, darkness, everyone distracted."

"Indeed," Santos said, watching her closely. "You've given this some thought."

"I'm a private investigator," Mallory reminded him. "Observation and analysis are part of the job."

After being released, Mallory found Tucker in the lobby, speaking with Vivian Harrington. The hotel owner's composure had finally cracked. Her face was pale with shock and distress.

"Two deaths in one day," she was saying, her voice barely audible over the continuing storm outside. "This can't be happening again."

"Again?" Tucker asked gently.

Vivian seemed to catch herself, straightening her shoulders with visible effort. "I simply meant... such tragedy. The hotel has seen its share over the years, but this..." she trailed off, looking toward where police officers were cordoning off the kitchen area. "I should check on my staff. They'll be distraught."

As Vivian moved away, Mallory joined Tucker. "Santos is suspicious of us," she murmured.

"With good reason," Tucker acknowledged. "We keep turning up at crime scenes. But I think he has bigger concerns now. Two murders in one day suggests urgency. It appears someone is tying up some loose ends."

"Or creating distractions," Mallory said. "The storm, the power outage, the confusion. It's the perfect cover for searching Room 118 or other areas without being noticed."

Tucker nodded. "I think we'd better check our room. If

someone is looking for Blackwood's research, they might think we have it."

They made their way upstairs, the emergency lighting casting long shadows in the hallways. Their suite appeared undisturbed at first glance, but Tucker's methodical inspection revealed subtle signs of intrusion: a drawer closed slightly differently than they had left it. The angle of Mallory's hairbrush on the vanity changed by a few degrees.

"Someone's been here," he said quietly. "Professional, thorough, but definitely here."

Mallory checked her hiding places. "The map fragment is still secure," she reported. "And the safe deposit box key."

"They might not have known exactly what they were looking for," Tucker said. "Maybe they were hoping to find Blackwood's research or notes."

A knock at their door interrupted their discussion. Tucker approached cautiously, checking through the peephole before opening it.

Cordelia Winters stood in the hallway, her expression grave. "May I come in? I believe we need to talk."

8

SUSPECTS AND MOTIVES

TUCKER HESITATED FOR A MOMENT, THEN STEPPED ASIDE TO allow Cordelia Winters into their suite. The novelist entered, her usual dramatic appearance subdued by the emergency lighting and the gravity of circumstances.

"I imagine you're wondering why I'm here," she said without preamble.

"The thought had crossed our minds," Mallory replied, studying the older woman carefully.

She was dressed impeccably in an emerald green knee-length sheath.

Cordelia moved to the sitting area and settled into one of the armchairs with practiced elegance. "Two deaths in one day tend to clarify one's priorities," she said, crossing her legs. "I've been researching the Harrington Hotel's history for my next novel, but I've uncovered more than I anticipated; information that may be relevant to what's happening now."

Tucker exchanged a glance with Mallory before they joined her, taking seats on the sofa across from her. "We're listening," he said.

"I know you're both investigators," Cordelia began. "And that your discovery of these deaths is no coincidence. You've been asking questions, examining Room 118, looking into the connection between Edwin's murder and Isabella Cruz's death forty years ago."

"You seem well-informed," Tucker said neutrally.

A smile flickered briefly across Cordelia's face. "Writers observe. It's our stock in trade. And small hotels are perfect petri dishes of human behavior; everyone watching everyone else, currents of suspicion and alliance flowing beneath polite conversation."

"And what have you discovered about the current situation?" Mallory asked.

"That we're approaching a significant date," Cordelia replied. "February 16th; the alignment Edwin was so excited about. The date when, according to Captain Harrington's journals, the shadows reveal the location of whatever he hid on this property."

"You knew about the alignment theory?" Tucker asked, not entirely surprised.

"Edwin shared his research with me," Cordelia acknowledged. "Initially because I expressed literary interest, but eventually because he needed someone to confide in. Someone outside the usual circle of suspects, if you will."

"And what exactly did he confide?" Mallory pressed.

Cordelia's expression grew more serious. "That he had discovered documents proving the Harrington family's wealth was founded on theft and murder. That Captain James Harrington didn't merely salvage Spanish artifacts, he killed the original salvagers and stole their findings. And that proof of this crime, along with the most valuable artifacts, was hidden somewhere on the property, its location encoded in an architectural feature that aligns only once every forty years."

"And the next alignment is in two days," Tucker said.

"Yes," Cordelia said. "Edwin believed Isabella Cruz discovered part of this secret during the renovations in 1985; the last time the alignment occurred. She was killed before she could reveal what she'd found. And now history is repeating itself with Edwin's murder. And Chef Dupont's."

"Why Dupont?" Mallory questioned. "What was his connection?"

"He and Edwin were close friends and fellow collectors," Cordelia explained. "Pierre helped authenticate some of the documents Edwin found, using his contacts in historical culinary circles to date food references and preparation methods mentioned in the journals."

"Was he killed for what he knew, or what he had?" Tucker asked.

"Possibly both," Cordelia replied. "Edwin trusted Pierre with information about his discoveries. And Pierre himself had acquired several smaller artifacts over the years, items with potential connections to the Harrington collection."

"Such as?" Mallory asked.

"A compass believed to belong to one of the Spanish sailors from the 1715 fleet. A silver serving piece with the Harrington crest that predated the hotel's construction. Things that raised questions about their provenance."

Tucker leaned forward slightly, his elbows on his knees, hands clasped together in front of him. "Why are you telling us this now, Ms. Winters?" He stared at her, his eyes narrowed.

Cordelia held his gaze, tilted her head slightly, then said, "Because two people are dead, and I have no desire to be the third. I came to the Harrington for research, but I've stumbled into something deadlier than I anticipated. You two are investigators with relevant experience and no obvious connection to the hotel's history. You're my best hope for getting out of here alive, and perhaps even getting the full story for my book."

"Self-preservation and professional research," Mallory said with a hint of skepticism. "Any other motivations we should know about?"

A flicker of appreciation crossed Cordelia's face. "You're very perceptive, Mrs. Randall. Yes, there's more. Years ago, I worked with Elaine Kincaid—before she married the judge. We were both researchers for an antiquities hunter named Harrison Blackwood."

"Any relation to Edwin?" Tucker asked sharply.

"His uncle," Cordelia said. "Harrison was obsessed with the 1715 fleet. He spent his life searching for remains of the missing ships. He had a particular theory about Captain Harrington's salvage operation. His theory was that Harrington had recovered far more than was ever officially documented. Harrison Blackwood died in a diving accident twelve years ago, still searching. Edwin inherited his research and continued the work."

"And Elaine?" Mallory asked.

"Moved on to more lucrative pursuits," Cordelia said dryly. "She married Judge Kincaid within six months of Harrison's death. The judge's interest in maritime law and salvage rights aligned conveniently with her expertise in Spanish colonial treasures."

Tucker processed this information. The connections were becoming clearer. "So we have Edwin Blackwood continuing his uncle's research into the Harrington treasure. Judge Kincaid and his wife Elaine, who has specialized knowledge of the subject. Gregory Marsh, an antiques dealer with a wealthy client interested in the 1715 fleet…" He paused, gave her a thin smile, then continued. "And you, researching for a novel, but with prior connections to all the key players."

"Don't forget Vivian Harrington," Cordelia said. "She's the

last of her family line, and the guardian of whatever secrets the hotel holds."

"And Detective Santos," Mallory said. "Whose mother has worked at the hotel for forty years, including when Isabella Cruz was killed."

"Quite the cast of characters," Cordelia said. "All with potential motives, all with something to gain or lose depending on what's revealed during the upcoming alignment."

"The question is which of them has resorted to murder," Tucker said.

"Or which ones, plural," Mallory said. "We could be dealing with multiple actors with different agendas."

Cordelia nodded. "That's my assessment as well. The timing of these deaths—just days before the alignment—can't be coincidence. Someone is eliminating people who know too much or who might interfere with their plans for February 16th."

"What exactly did Edwin believe would be revealed during the alignment?" Tucker asked.

"A location," Cordelia replied. "Somewhere on the property where Captain Harrington hid both the most valuable artifacts and documents incriminating him in their theft. Edwin had partially decoded journal entries suggesting that the original hiding place was the old family cemetery, but that items were moved during hotel renovations in the early 1900s."

"To the east wing," Mallory surmised. "Where Room 118 is now."

"Possibly," Cordelia acknowledged. "Though Edwin's latest theory involved the basement level. He'd found references to structural changes that don't appear in any official blueprints."

Tucker stood and moved to the window, watching the

storm still raging outside. The power outage, originally confined to the hotel, now appeared to affect the surrounding area as well; the lights of St. Augustine were dimmed or absent entirely.

"Ms. Winters," he said, turning back to her, "why should we trust you? By your own admission, you have connections to multiple suspects and a professional interest in this mystery."

Cordelia smiled thinly. "You shouldn't trust me completely," she said. "That would be foolish. But consider this; if I wanted whatever is hidden here, would I reveal what I know to two experienced investigators? Would I draw attention to my own connections and potential motives?"

"Unless that's exactly your strategy," Mallory pointed out. "Appearing forthcoming to avoid suspicion."

"A fair point," Cordelia said. "I can only say that I value my life more than any treasure, and my literary success more than any artifacts. A bestselling novel about these events— written from a safe distance once the danger has passed— serves my interests better than risking murder charges."

Before either Tucker or Mallory could respond, a sharp knock on their door interrupted the conversation. Tucker approached cautiously, checking through the peephole again.

"Detective Santos," he murmured to Mallory before opening the door.

The detective stood in the hallway, his expression grim in the emergency lighting. "Mr. Randall. Mrs. Randall." His gaze shifted to Cordelia. "Ms. Winters. I need to speak with all of you."

"Come in, Detective," Tucker invited, stepping aside.

Santos entered, scanning the room briefly before focusing on the three of them. "The medical examiner has made a preliminary determination on Chef Dupont's death. It was not an accident. He was struck on the back of the head and then locked in the freezer while unconscious."

"Murder," Mallory said quietly. "Like Blackwood."

"Yes," Santos said. "And given the timing and circumstances, we believe the cases are connected."

"Have you identified any suspects?" Tucker asked.

Santos' expression revealed nothing. "We're pursuing several lines of inquiry. Including why Chef Dupont requested to see you two specifically just before his death."

"We told you," Mallory said. "He sent our server with a message to meet him in the kitchen. We assumed it was about rescheduling our tour."

"So you said," Santos acknowledged. "However, your server Megan has no recollection of delivering such a message."

Tucker and Mallory exchanged a surprised glance. "That's not possible," Tucker said. "She came directly to our table with the message."

"Unless," Cordelia interjected, "it wasn't Megan who delivered it."

Santos turned his attention to her. "Explain."

"The power was out," Cordelia pointed out. "Emergency lighting only. Staff moving around in unfamiliar patterns due to the disruption. It would be relatively easy for someone to impersonate a server, deliver a message, and thereby lure them to discover another body."

Santos considered this. "And why would someone want you to find Chef Dupont's body?"

"To implicate us," Tucker said. "We already found Blackwood. Finding Dupont as well makes us look suspicious."

"Or to ensure the body was found promptly," Mallory said. "Before the freezer could do too much damage and obscure evidence."

Santos' gaze moved between them, assessing. "You've given this considerable thought."

"It's what we do," Tucker reminded him. "We're investigators."

After a moment, Santos nodded. "I need statements from all of you regarding your whereabouts during the power outage. And I'd appreciate it if you'd refrain from discussing these deaths with other guests. We're trying to maintain some semblance of control over the investigation."

"Of course," Tucker said. "We're happy to cooperate."

After taking their statements, Santos departed, leaving them to consider the implications of this latest development.

"Someone set you up," Cordelia said once the detective was gone. "They used the confusion of the power outage to eliminate Dupont and implicate you in the process."

"The question is who," Mallory said. "And why they're killing now, so close to the alignment date? If they wanted to prevent discovery of whatever is hidden here, wouldn't it make more sense to wait until after February 16th had passed?"

"Unless they need to find it first," Tucker said. "So they eliminate those who know too much, then use the alignment to locate the cache themselves."

"Which brings us back to our list of suspects," Cordelia said. "Each with their own motive to find what's hidden and eliminate competition."

"We need to narrow it down," Tucker said. "Starting tomorrow, we focus on connecting concrete evidence to specific suspects."

"We should check out the old cemetery Ruiz mentioned," Mallory said. "If that was the original hiding place, there might still be clues there."

Cordelia rose to leave. "I should go before Santos returns with more questions. But I'd like to propose an alliance. I'll share what I know, you share what you discover, and together we might survive long enough to solve this mystery."

Tucker and Mallory exchanged a glance, one of their silent communications that had become second nature over their years of partnership.

"Okay," Tucker said finally. "But with the understanding that our priority is stopping these killings, not finding treasure."

"Fair enough," Cordelia replied, moving toward the door. "Though in my experience, the two objectives are likely to converge. Whoever is killing to protect or acquire this secret won't stop until they have what they want, or until they're caught."

After she departed, Tucker secured the door and turned to Mallory. "What do you think? Can we trust her?"

"About sixty percent," Mallory replied. "She's holding something back, but her fear seems genuine. And her literary ambition provides a plausible motive for cooperation."

"We'll verify whatever she tells us," Tucker said. "And in the meantime, we take precautions. No splitting up, no meetings alone with any of our suspects, and we secure this room as best we can."

Outside, the storm continued unabated, wind and rain lashing against their windows like nature itself was trying to break in and uncover the secrets hidden within the Harrington Hotel's walls.

9

THE OLD MURDER

MORNING ARRIVED WITH LINGERING EVIDENCE OF THE NIGHT'S storm—fallen palm fronds scattered across the hotel grounds, sand washed up onto the walkways, and a moody gray sky that promised more rain to come. The power had been restored sometime during the night, but the hotel staff still moved with the heightened alertness of people operating in crisis mode.

Tucker woke early to find Mallory already up and dressed in jeans and white blouse, typing notes on her phone by the window.

He rolled over onto his side, propped himself up on his elbow, and watched her for a moment, admiring her silhouette in the window's light. And he had one of those moments when his heart seemed to skip a beat. *She's so... lovely*, he thought.

"I can feel you staring at me," she said without looking up from her phone.

"Good morning," he said, throwing off the covers and swinging his feet to floor. It was then he remembered he was naked and was for a moment embarrassed, but the moment passed when he remembered he was also married to the beautiful woman sitting at the window. He picked his shorts up off the floor and quickly slipped them on.

"There's no need to be shy," she said, still without looking up.

"I'm not shy," he muttered. "What time is it?"

"Just after eight," she replied.

"Really? Oh hell. Why didn't you wake me?"

He stepped up behind her, bent over, his cheek against hers, slipped his arms around her and nuzzled her. She turned her face to his and kissed him. "Go take a shower," she said. "Then we can go get some breakfast." She kissed him again. He nodded, turned her loose and went to the bathroom. Twenty minutes later, he was dressed in a pair of white golf pants and a very pale pink golf shirt.

"I checked the weather report," she said when he joined her at the window. "The storm's moved north, but they're predicting more rain throughout the day. It's the perfect time for visiting a bank and an old cemetery."

Tucker nodded. "Sounds like a plan," he said. "But breakfast first. I'm starving."

"Me, too," she said as she stood up. "Let's go." And together, they headed downstairs for breakfast.

The dining room was subdued, with fewer guests than the previous morning. News of Chef Dupont's death had spread, and many families with children had apparently chosen to cut their stays short despite the hotel's assurances about safety.

Detective Santos was in the lobby, speaking with two uniformed officers. He acknowledged Tucker and Mallory with a slight nod as they passed, but made no move to intercept them.

"He's watching us," Mallory murmured as they found a

table. "Not interfering yet, but definitely keeping an eye on us."

"Good," Tucker replied quietly. "Better to have him where we can see him, too."

They ordered breakfast from a somber-faced server—not Megan, they both noticed—and used the meal to outline their plan for the day.

"Coastal Bank opens at nine," Tucker said, checking his watch. "If we leave now, we should be there shortly after nine-thirty. Then we find Ruiz and ask about the cemetery."

"What about Room 118?" Mallory asked. "Should we check to see if anything's changed there?"

Tucker considered this. "Too risky during daylight hours, with police still on the property. We'll try again tonight if necessary, depending on what we learn from the safe deposit box."

They finished their meal quickly and were heading for the front entrance when Elaine Kincaid intercepted them, looking immaculate in a tailored white, sleeveless jumpsuit despite the upheavals.

"Mr. and Mrs. Randall," she greeted them with a practiced smile. "Venturing out despite the weather? You're braver than I am."

"Just some honeymoon shopping," Mallory replied smoothly. "We can't let a little rain ruin our plans."

"Of course not," Elaine said, her eyes assessing them carefully. "Though I'd have thought yesterday's events might have dampened your enthusiasm for exploration."

"Life goes on," Tucker said neutrally. "Even after a tragedy."

Something flickered in Elaine's expression: approval, perhaps, or calculation. "Indeed it does," she replied. "Walter and I were just discussing that very philosophy over breakfast. He's quite fascinated by how this hotel has endured through the various... unfortunate incidents over the years."

"Including Isabella Cruz's murder?" Mallory asked.

If Elaine was surprised by the blunt question, she didn't show it. "Among others," she said. "Walter has researched several cases connected to historic properties for his book. The psychological impact of violence on a location. How it becomes part of the fabric of a place."

"Interesting perspective," Tucker commented. "More philosophical than legal."

"Yes, my husband is indeed philosophical," Elaine replied with a small smile. "He's not merely the stern jurist people perceive. His interest in history has emotional dimensions as well."

"And your interest?" Mallory asked. "You worked in antiquities research before your marriage, I understand."

Again, that slight flicker in Elaine's expression, recognition that they knew more than she'd expected. "I did. With Harrison Blackwood, Edwin's uncle. Small world, isn't it? Though my focus was academic, not commercial. The historical significance rather than monetary value."

"Of course," Tucker said, his tone suggesting no judgment either way.

"Well, I won't keep you from your shopping," Elaine said, clearly bringing the conversation to an end. "Though you might want to take an umbrella. The weather report suggests another squall moving in by midday."

As she walked away, Mallory murmured, "She was fishing for information about where we're going."

"And now she knows we know her connection to Harrison Blackwood," Tucker said.

"Layers within layers," Mallory muttered. "Let's get to that bank before anyone else decides to chat."

The rain had temporarily subsided as they exited the

hotel, but dark clouds on the horizon confirmed Elaine's weather prediction. They walked briskly through St. Augustine's historic district, the normally bustling streets relatively quiet in the storm's aftermath.

The Coastal Bank was housed in a modest building of coral-colored stucco with white trim, set between a gift shop and a small cafe on King Street. A security guard nodded to them as they entered; it was nine-thirty-five.

Tucker approached the receptionist, presenting the safe deposit box key and the information from Blackwood's letter. "We need to access box 247, registered to James Carpenter."

The receptionist checked their identification and verified the information against the bank's records. "Do you have the password as well, Mr. Randall?"

Tucker exchanged a glance with Mallory. Blackwood's letter had mentioned his birth date as secondary identification, but not a password. "Would it be his date of birth?" he guessed.

The receptionist checked her screen again. "I'm afraid not. Without the password, I can't authorize access to the box."

"What about executor authorization?" Mallory said. "In the event of the box holder's death?"

"That would require legal documentation—a death certificate and proof of executor status," the receptionist explained patiently.

Tucker considered their options. They had the key, which Blackwood had clearly intended them to use, but not the password or legal standing to access the box otherwise.

"Is there a manager we could speak with?" he asked. "This is a somewhat unusual situation."

The receptionist made a call, and a few minutes later, an older man in a conservative suit appeared from a back office.

"I'm Howard Keene, the bank manager. I understand there's an issue with a safe deposit box?"

Tucker explained the situation—that Edwin Blackwood had left the key with instructions to access the box, but they didn't have the password.

"Mr. Blackwood is deceased?" Keene asked, his expression grave.

"Yes," Mallory said. "He was found murdered yesterday morning at the Harrington Hotel."

Keene's eyebrows rose. "I see. And you are…?"

"Private investigators," Tucker explained. "We believe the contents of this box may contain information relevant to his murder."

"Have you spoken with the police?" Keene asked. "A court order would allow us to open the box."

"We're cooperating with Detective Santos," Mallory assured him. "But given the urgency of the situation—a second murder occurred last night—we were hoping to expedite the process."

Keene considered this, clearly weighing bank protocol against the extraordinary circumstances. "The account is registered under a pseudonym, you say?"

"James Carpenter," Tucker said. "Blackwood's maternal grandfather, according to his letter."

Something in this detail seemed to resonate with Keene. "One moment, please." He disappeared into his office, returning a few minutes later with a folder. "Mr. Blackwood opened this account three years ago. He indicated that in the event of emergency access being needed, the password could be found by combining the middle names of Captain James Harrington's three children."

Tucker and Mallory exchanged a frustrated glance. "We don't have that information," Tucker admitted.

"However," Keene continued, "he also said that the information could be found in a specific book in the St. Augustine Historical Society's library—'Maritime Families of Florida's First Coast,' page 142."

"The historical society," Mallory repeated. "How far is that from here?"

"Three blocks south," Keene replied. "On Aviles Street. They open at ten o'clock."

Tucker checked his watch. "That gives us about twenty minutes. Thank you for your help, Mr. Keene. We'll return once we have the password."

Outside, the sky had darkened further, and a light drizzle had begun. They set a brisk pace toward the historical society, discussing their next steps.

"Blackwood was thorough," Mallory said. "Creating a trail that only someone investigating his death would follow."

"And using Captain Harrington's children's names as the password," Tucker said. "Connecting the contents directly to the family's history."

The St. Augustine Historical Society was housed in a Spanish colonial building with thick coquina walls and a small courtyard garden. Despite the inclement weather, a small line of tourists had already formed outside, waiting for the ten o'clock opening.

As they joined the queue, Tucker scanned their surroundings, an old habit from his FBI days. "We're being followed," he said quietly to Mallory. "Don't look now, but there's a man in a gray raincoat across the street, pretending to examine shop windows."

Mallory waited a moment, then casually turned as if taking in the historical architecture. "I see him. Not exactly subtle, is he?"

"Professional, but not top-tier," Tucker said. "Probably hoping the rain and crowd would provide enough cover."

"Gregory Marsh?" Mallory said. "Or someone working for him?"

"Possibly," Tucker replied. "Or Judge Kincaid."

The historical society's doors opened precisely at ten, and they filed in with the other visitors. While tourists headed for the main exhibition area, Tucker and Mallory made their way to the research library at the rear of the building.

The librarian, an elderly woman with wire-rimmed glasses and a cardigan despite the Florida climate, looked up from her desk as they approached.

"We need to locate a specific book," Tucker explained. "'Maritime Families of Florida's First Coast.' It's for research into the Harrington Hotel's history."

The mention of the Harrington seemed to pique the librarian's interest. "The Harrington, you say? Interesting timing, with poor Edwin's death yesterday. Terrible business."

"You knew Mr. Blackwood?" Mallory asked.

"Everyone in St. Augustine's historical community knew Edwin," the librarian replied. "He was a regular here, always deep in research about the Harrington family and their connection to the 1715 fleet." She rose from her desk. "Maritime Families is in our reference section. I'll show you."

As they followed her through the stacks, Tucker kept an eye on the library entrance. Their follower hadn't entered yet, perhaps waiting outside to avoid being too obvious.

"Here we are," the librarian said, pulling a large leather-bound volume from a shelf. "Comprehensive genealogies of the major maritime families of northeastern Florida. The Harringtons are well documented, given their prominence in salvage operations."

She placed the book on a nearby table and left them to their research. Tucker quickly turned to page 142, finding a detailed family tree of the Harrington line. Captain James

Harrington and his wife Elizabeth had three children: William Thomas Harrington, Mary Louise Harrington, and James Frederick Harrington.

"The middle names," Mallory said. "Thomas, Louise, Frederick. That must be the password."

Tucker recorded the information in his phone. "Let's get back to the bank."

As they prepared to leave, the librarian approached again. "Did you find what you needed?"

"Yes, thank you," Tucker replied. "The Harrington genealogy is quite extensive."

"Indeed," she said. "Though not always accurately represented. Family histories tend to… omit certain unflattering details."

Mallory frowned. Something in her tone said deeper knowledge. "Such as?" Mallory asked.

The librarian glanced around, though the library was nearly empty. "Edwin was investigating connections between the Harrington family and certain disappearances that occurred during salvage operations. Rival salvagers who went missing after claiming to have found Spanish wrecks in areas the Harringtons considered their territory."

"Murder?" Tucker asked quietly.

"It was never proven," the librarian replied. "But Edwin found court records suggesting Captain Harrington was questioned about at least three such disappearances. Nothing came of the investigations. The Harringtons were too powerful locally."

"Was this public knowledge?" Mallory asked.

"Hardly," she replied. "Those court records were sealed until forty years ago. Edwin only discovered them recently." She adjusted her glasses. "He was quite excited about some connection to Isabella Cruz's murder, though he didn't share the details with me."

Tucker and Mallory exchanged a glance. "Thank you for the information," Tucker said. "It's very helpful."

"Just be careful," the librarian warned. "Edwin's questions about the Harrington family's past made certain people uncomfortable. And now he's dead."

Outside, the rain had intensified. Their shadow was still present, now sheltering under an awning across the street, his attention fixed on the historical society's entrance.

"Let's give him something to follow," Tucker murmured. They set off in the direction opposite to the bank, hurrying through the rain-slicked streets. After two blocks, they ducked into a small cafe.

"Coffee to go, please," Tucker requested at the counter. When the barista turned to prepare their order, he and Mallory slipped out the rear service entrance into an alley that ran behind the row of shops.

Moving rapidly but without obvious haste, they circled back toward Coastal Bank, approaching from the opposite direction. Their pursuer was nowhere in sight.

Mr. Keene was waiting when they returned to the bank. "Did you find the information?" he asked.

"ThomasLouiseFrederick," Tucker replied. "The middle names of Captain Harrington's children."

Keene nodded. "If you'll follow me, I'll take you to the vault."

The safe deposit box was smaller than Tucker had expected—roughly the size of a shoebox. Keene used his master key in conjunction with the key Blackwood had provided, then left them alone in a small private room to examine the contents.

Inside the box were several items: a leather-bound journal, a manila envelope containing what appeared to be photocopies of old documents, a small USB drive, and a brass key that was significantly older than the one for the safe deposit box itself.

"Where do we start?" Mallory asked, surveying the contents.

"The journal," Tucker said, carefully lifting it from the box.

The journal was well-worn, its pages filled with Blackwood's precise handwriting. It appeared to be a research log, documenting his investigation into the Harrington family and the 1715 fleet. The earliest entries dated back nearly three years.

"Listen to this," Tucker said, reading from an entry dated six months earlier. "'I finally located the Cruz case file through D.S.'s mother. Original detective deliberately overlooked evidence connecting death to east wing renovations. Witness statement from F.R. regarding suspicious activity night of murder was removed from the official record.'"

"D.S. would be Detective Santos," Mallory said. "And F.R. is Francisco Ruiz. So Santos' mother helped Blackwood access the original case file."

"Which suggests she might have suspicions about the official version too," Tucker said, continuing to scan the journal. "Here's another entry from two months ago: 'Architectural plans confirm the shadow theory. February 16th alignment will reveal the access point in the main staircase newel post. Captain's journals indicate secret compartment containing document cache and map to artifact repository.'"

"The main staircase," Mallory repeated. "Not Room 118 or the basement?"

"Apparently those were secondary locations," Tucker said, reading further. "Room 118 contained documents pointing to the staircase as the primary location. Blackwood found those, which is why he was killed."

"And the newel post will only reveal its secret during the

alignment on February 16th," Mallory said. "That's why the timing of these murders is so critical. The killer needs to eliminate anyone who knows about the alignment before it happens, then be positioned to access the newel post at the precise moment."

Tucker nodded, turning to the last entry in the journal, dated just three days before Blackwood's murder: "'Evidence connecting H family to Rojas murder conclusive. Captain's grandson confessed in private journal, now in V's possession. If genuine, it proves inheritance built on murder. Will confront V with findings tomorrow.'"

"V must be Vivian," Mallory said. "Blackwood was planning to confront her with evidence that her family's wealth came from murder."

"And the next day, he ended up dead," Tucker said grimly. "Timing suggests Vivian might be our killer."

"Or someone protecting her interests," Mallory said. "Someone who knew Blackwood was about to expose family secrets."

Tucker turned his attention to the manila envelope, carefully removing the photocopied documents inside. They appeared to be pages from Captain Harrington's personal journals, along with court records from the 1880s.

"These detail the disappearance of a salvager named Miguel Rojas," Tucker said, scanning the documents. "He claimed to have found the richest of the 1715 wrecks, then vanished days later. Captain Harrington subsequently reported finding the same wreck 'by chance' and recovered significant Spanish gold and artifacts."

"And according to Blackwood's notes, there's a confession connecting the Harrington family to Rojas's murder," Mallory said. "A journal in Vivian's possession that proves her family's fortune began with murder."

Tucker picked up the USB drive next. "We'll need a

computer to check this. And the brass key—I'm guessing it opens whatever is hidden in the newel post."

"Or something else entirely," Mallory said. "Blackwood was investigating multiple angles."

They carefully returned the items to the safe deposit box, except for the USB drive, the journal and brass key, which Tucker handed to Mallory. After thanking Mr. Keene for his help, they stepped outside to find the rain had temporarily subsided, though dark clouds still threatened overhead.

"Back to the hotel?" Mallory said. "We need to find Francisco Ruiz and ask about his witness statement."

Tucker nodded in agreement. "And we need to take a closer look at that main staircase. If the newel post is key to this mystery, we should examine it before the alignment tomorrow."

As they walked back toward the Harrington, Tucker couldn't shake the feeling that they were racing against time. With two people already dead, the killer had demonstrated both determination and ruthlessness. And with the crucial alignment now less than twenty-four hours away, the stakes would only increase.

The question now was whether they could identify the killer before someone else died—and whether the secrets hidden within the Harrington Hotel were truly worth killing for.

10

FAMILY SECRETS

THE HARRINGTON HOTEL APPEARED ODDLY SUBDUED WHEN Tucker and Mallory returned. The lobby, usually populated with guests and staff, was nearly empty except for a young man at the reception desk who seemed relieved by their arrival.

"Mr. and Mrs. Randall," he greeted them. "Detective Santos was asking for you earlier."

"Did he leave a message?" Tucker asked.

"He just asked to be notified when you returned," the clerk replied. "He's meeting with Ms. Harrington in her office now."

Tucker nodded. "We'll be in our room if he needs us."

As they crossed the lobby toward the grand staircase, Mallory slowed her pace, her attention fixed on the ornate newel post at the base of the stairs. The heavy wooden column was elaborately carved with maritime motifs—ropes, shells, and what appeared to be a small ship on the rounded cap.

"Hiding in plain sight," she murmured. "Everyone touches it, but no one really sees it."

Tucker studied the post with new interest. "No obvious way to open it. Must be a hidden mechanism that only works during the alignment."

"Or with this," Mallory said, touching her pocket where the brass key was secured.

They continued upstairs to their room, locking the door behind them. Tucker checked for signs of intrusion while Mallory opened her laptop.

"All clear," he reported after a thorough inspection. "Now, let's see what's on that USB drive."

The drive contained several files: digital photographs of documents too fragile to photocopy, scans of architectural blueprints for the Harrington Hotel's original construction in 1872, and a detailed analysis of celestial alignments as they related to the property's orientation.

"Blackwood was thorough," Mallory said, opening a file labeled 'Alignment Theory.' It contained a series of diagrams showing how, on February 16th, the sun would create a specific shadow pattern through a particular window, highlighting the newel post for approximately three minutes between 10:12 and 10:15 AM.

"Look at this," Tucker said, pointing to another diagram. "The shadow creates a specific pattern that reveals a keyhole."

"And it's hidden the rest of the time," Mallory said. "What a clever design. You'd need both the knowledge of when the alignment occurs and the key to access whatever's inside."

"And tomorrow morning is the only time it works," Tucker said. "Exactly forty years after Isabella Cruz was killed."

A knock at their door interrupted their examination of the files. Tucker approached cautiously, checking through the peephole to see Detective Santos standing in the hallway.

"Detective," Tucker greeted him as he opened the door. "You want to see us?"

Santos' expression was unreadable as he entered the room. "I understand you two left the hotel early this morning," he said. "D'you mind telling me where you went?"

"We went shopping, like we mentioned to Ms. Kincaid," Mallory replied smoothly. "Though the weather cut our plans short."

Santos' gaze flickered to the laptop screen, where the alignment diagrams were still visible. "Shopping for historical documents about the Harrington Hotel?" he asked.

Tucker exchanged a glance with Mallory, then made a decision. "Detective, we haven't been entirely forthcoming. We've been investigating connections between Edwin Blackwood's murder and Isabella Cruz's death forty years ago."

"I'm aware," Santos replied dryly. "You haven't been as subtle as you might think."

"Then you also know that both deaths are connected to something hidden in this hotel," Mallory said. "Something that can only be accessed during a specific alignment that occurs tomorrow morning."

Santos studied them both for a long moment. "My mother worked here when Isabella Cruz was killed," he said. "She never believed the official story about a random intruder. There were too many coincidences, too many details that didn't add up."

"Did she share those concerns with you?" Tucker asked.

"Not until recently," Santos admitted. "When Edwin started asking questions, digging into the old case files, my mother finally told me what she suspected, that Isabella found something during the renovations that the Harrington family wanted kept secret."

"Something valuable?" Mallory asked.

"Something incriminating," Santos corrected. "Documentation proving that the Harrington fortune was founded on theft and murder. Captain James Harrington allegedly killed a rival salvager named Miguel Rojas and stole his find of Spanish gold."

Tucker nodded. "That matches what we found in Blackwood's research. He believed he'd located evidence confirming this theory, including a confession in the private journal of Captain Harrington's grandson."

"A journal now in Vivian Harrington's possession," Santos said. "Blackwood approached my mother about it three days before his death. He'd traced the journal's provenance to Vivian's personal collection."

"Did he confront Vivian?" Mallory asked.

"According to my mother, he intended to," Santos replied. "He wanted to verify the journal's authenticity before going public with his findings."

"And the next day, he wound up dead in the tide pool," Tucker said. "Which makes Vivian our prime suspect."

Santos shook his head. "It's not that simple. Vivian has an alibi for the estimated time of Blackwood's death. She was on a video call with the hotel's corporate board until 1 AM, then spoke with the night clerk until nearly 2 AM. The medical examiner places Blackwood's death between midnight and 2 AM."

"Could she have hired someone?" Mallory asked.

"Possible, but unlikely given the personal nature of the confrontation Blackwood was planning," Santos replied. "More importantly, Vivian seemed genuinely shocked when I questioned her about the journal. She claims no knowledge of its existence in her collection."

"She could be lying," Tucker said.

"She could," Santos replied. "But that brings us to Chef Dupont's murder. Vivian was in the dining room throughout the power outage, visible to multiple witnesses. She couldn't have killed him."

"So either we're looking at two different killers," Mallory said, thoughtfully, "or someone else has a motive to protect the Harrington family secrets."

"Or create a distraction while they search for the treasure themselves," Tucker said. "What about Judge Kincaid and his wife? Or Gregory Marsh?"

"All had opportunity during the power outage," Santos said. "Kincaid left his table briefly, claiming he needed to use the restroom. Marsh disappeared entirely for about fifteen minutes. And Cordelia Winters went to 'check on a manuscript' in her room."

"All suspects with motives related to either the treasure or the historical documentation," Tucker said. "Kincaid researching maritime law and salvage rights, Marsh representing a wealthy collector, Winters writing a book about the Harrington mystery."

"And all of them asking questions about the February 16th date," Santos said. "My officers have reported multiple guests expressing specific interest in the main staircase and its architectural features."

Mallory looked surprised. "You know about the newel post?"

Santos nodded. "My mother told me about Captain Harrington's design innovations. The alignment, the hidden compartment, all of it. Family legend passed down through hotel staff who've been here for generations."

"Then you know that whatever is hidden there will be accessible tomorrow morning," Tucker said. "Between 10:12 and 10:15 AM."

"I know," Santos said. "And I've arranged for additional officers to be present, though discreetly. Whatever happens, I intend to ensure no one else dies over this century-old secret."

Tucker and Mallory exchanged a glance.

"Detective," Tucker said finally, "we have information that might help identify the killer. Blackwood left a research journal in a safe deposit box, accessible only through a series of clues. We retrieved it this morning." He removed the journal from his pocket and handed it to Santos.

The detective accepted it with raised eyebrows. "I appreciate your cooperation. Though I have to wonder why you're sharing this now."

"Because two people are already dead," Mallory explained. "And whoever killed them is still here, waiting for tomorrow's alignment. We want to stop them before anyone else gets hurt."

Santos nodded, leafing through the journal. "This contains specific accusations about the Harrington family's criminal history," he said. "Publication would devastate their reputation and potentially expose them to legal consequences, even after all this time."

"A powerful motive," Tucker said. "The question is, who feels strongly enough about protecting that secret to commit murder?"

"Or who wants to exploit it for their own gain?" Mallory said.

Santos closed the journal and fixed them with a serious look. "I want you both to be careful. You've been asking questions. The killer must realize you're getting close."

"We will," Tucker said. "But we need to talk to Francisco Ruiz. According to Blackwood's notes, Ruiz gave a witness statement about suspicious activity the night of Isabella Cruz's murder, a statement that was removed from the official record."

"I've been looking for Mr. Ruiz all morning," Santos said.

"He didn't report for work today, and he's not in his cottage on the grounds."

Alarm bells went off in Tucker's mind. "That's concerning," he said. "Especially given what happened to Blackwood and Dupont."

"I have officers checking local hospitals and his known associates," Santos said. "So far, nothing."

"We need to find him," Mallory said. "He's one of only a few living witnesses from the original murder who might have seen something."

Santos nodded in agreement. "In the meantime," he said. "I suggest you both remain in the public areas of the hotel. The killer has shown they're willing to isolate their victims."

"We'll be careful," Tucker said. "And we'll let you know if we find anything else relevant in Blackwood's files."

After Santos departed with the journal, Tucker locked the door and turned to Mallory. "He knows more than he's saying."

"Absolutely," Mallory said. "He's investigating, but he's also protecting something... or someone."

"His mother, maybe?" Tucker replied. "She's worked here for forty years. She was also friends with Isabella Cruz and apparently knew about the alignment secret all along."

"But she never told her son until recently," Mallory said. "That's significant. Why keep it secret from him, especially since he's in law enforcement?"

"Professional boundaries, perhaps," Tucker said. "Or maybe she was protecting herself in some way."

"We need to talk to her," Mallory said. "And find Ruiz. I'm worried about his sudden disappearance."

Tucker checked his watch. "It's nearly noon. Let's head down to lunch and see if we can locate Gloria Mendez. As head housekeeper, she should be overseeing the dining room preparations."

As they prepared to leave, Mallory paused by the window, looking out at the hotel grounds where workers were cleaning up storm debris. "Tucker," she said slowly, "do you see that area beyond the formal gardens? That overgrown section with what looks like stone markers?"

Tucker joined her. In the distance, partially obscured by trees and untended foliage, he could make out what appeared to be small monuments or headstones. "The old Harrington cemetery Ruiz mentioned," he said. "Where Captain Harrington's original cache might have been hidden."

"And where Francisco Ruiz might have gone if he was looking for evidence connected to Isabella's murder," Mallory said. "It's worth checking out."

Tucker nodded in agreement. "After lunch. We'll approach it casually, like honeymooners exploring the grounds. We'll be less likely to attract attention that way."

As they headed downstairs, Tucker couldn't shake a growing sense of unease. With Ruiz missing and the crucial alignment less than twenty-four hours away, the investigation was approaching its climax. The killer had already struck twice to protect secrets hidden for forty years, or perhaps for over a century, if Captain Harrington's original crimes were indeed the root of it all.

11

THE HISTORIAN'S NOTES

THE HOTEL DINING ROOM WAS SUBDUED DURING LUNCH. WITH Chef Dupont's death still fresh in everyone's minds and several guests having departed after the double tragedy, the normally bustling space felt hollow. A sous chef had taken over kitchen operations, offering a simplified menu that seemed fitting for the somber atmosphere.

Tucker and Mallory selected a table with a good view of both the entrance and the kitchen doors, positioning themselves to observe without being obvious. Gregory Marsh was dining alone near the windows, occasionally checking his phone with some impatience. The Kincaids had not yet appeared, nor had Cordelia Winters.

"I'm concerned about Ruiz," Mallory murmured as they awaited their food. "His disappearance right before the alignment can't be coincidence."

"Agreed," Tucker replied quietly. "Best-case scenario, he's gone into hiding to protect himself. Worst case..."

He didn't need to finish the thought. They both knew that if the killer had realized Ruiz was a potential witness who could connect dots across forty years, he might have become their third victim.

Their server arrived with their meals, simple sandwiches that bore little resemblance to yesterday's more elaborate cuisine. As she set down their plates, Tucker noticed her name tag: Megan.

"Excuse me," he said. "You're Megan, correct? You served us yesterday at dinner?"

The young woman nodded, looking slightly nervous. "Yes, sir."

"Detective Santos mentioned you had no recollection of delivering a message to us from Chef Dupont," Tucker continued in a calm, non-accusatory tone. "We're just trying to understand what happened."

Megan glanced around, then lowered her voice. "I never delivered any message. I was working the other side of the dining room during the power outage. Someone else must have come to your table pretending to be me."

"Can you tell us about the servers who were working last night?" Mallory asked.

"There were five of us," Megan replied. "Me, Margo, Julie, Ann and Maria. We all wear the same uniform. It would have been easy for someone to borrow one from the dirties in the basket in the break room, especially in the darkness."

"Did you notice anyone unusual in or near the kitchen during the outage?" Tucker asked.

Megan hesitated. "I saw Ms. Kincaid near the service entrance at one point. She said she was looking for the restroom, but that area is clearly marked 'Staff Only.'"

Tucker and Mallory exchanged a glance. "Thank you, Megan," Mallory said.

After the server departed, they ate quickly while discussing this new information in hushed tones.

"Elaine Kincaid was near the kitchen during the power

outage," Tucker said. "And we know she has expertise in antiquities from her work with Harrison Blackwood."

"Plus her convenient marriage to a judge researching maritime salvage law," Mallory said. "The timing of that has always seemed suspicious to me."

"We need to look more closely at the Kincaids," Tucker said. "And we still need to find Gloria Mendez and check the old cemetery."

As if on cue, they spotted Gloria entering the dining room, speaking with a staff member while gesturing toward various tables that needed attention. Her authority over the housekeeping staff was clear in their quick responses to her directions.

Tucker caught her eye and nodded slightly, indicating they wanted to speak with her. After a moment's hesitation, Gloria approached their table.

"Mr. and Mrs. Randall," she greeted them formally. "Is everything satisfactory?"

"Very much so," Tucker assured her. "We were actually hoping to speak with you about the hotel's history. Detective Santos mentioned you've worked here for many years."

Gloria's expression revealed nothing, but her posture stiffened slightly. "Forty-three years," she said. "Since I was seventeen."

"So you were here when Isabella Cruz worked at the Harrington," Mallory said.

Gloria glanced around the dining room, then back at them. "This is not a good place to discuss such matters," she said quietly. "Meet me in the linen closet on your floor in thirty minutes. It's at the end of the hall, opposite the ice machine." Then she turned and walked quickly to another table.

"Interesting," Mallory said.

Tucker smiled but said nothing.

They finished their meal and left the dining room. As they entered the lobby, they saw Cordelia Winters descending the grand staircase, her attention fixed on the ornate newel post at its base. When she spotted them, she altered course.

"Our historian's notes have proven illuminating, haven't they?" she asked quietly as she joined them near a display of fresh flowers. "The patterns all point to tomorrow morning."

"You know about the alignment," Tucker said, not entirely surprised.

"Edwin shared his theories with me," Cordelia said. "Not all the details, of course, but enough. The newel post, the February 16th date, the shadow pattern that reveals what's hidden."

"Did he share this information with anyone else?" Mallory asked.

"Judge Kincaid, certainly," Cordelia replied. "They had several intense discussions about maritime salvage laws and how they might apply to artifacts hidden on the property. And I believe Vivian knows more than she lets on. Edwin mentioned confronting her with his findings shortly before his death."

"Have you seen Francisco Ruiz today? He seems to have disappeared."

"No," Cordelia replied, looking genuinely concerned. "That's worrying, given recent events. The gardener who knows too much going missing just before the alignment? Another loose end being tied up, perhaps."

"We're thinking the same thing," Tucker acknowledged. "We're planning to check out the old Harrington cemetery after our meeting. Ruiz mentioned it when we talked to him yesterday. "

"The old cemetery? I've seen it from my window," Cordelia said. "It's overgrown, abandoned. If you're going there, I'd like to join you. Safety in numbers, and I might recognize historical contexts you'd miss."

Tucker considered the offer. Having another person along reduced the risk of being isolated by the killer, but only if Cordelia herself wasn't involved. Still, her knowledge of historical details could prove valuable.

"Meet us in the lobby at two o'clock," he said. "And it's bound to be muddy out there, so dress accordingly."

After Cordelia departed, they made their way upstairs, timing their arrival at the linen closet to match Gloria's thirty-minute window. The small room was cramped but private and filled with shelves of folded sheets and towels.

Gloria was already there, her expression grave as she closed the door behind them.

"You're asking dangerous questions," she began without preamble. "Two people are already dead because of what's hidden in this hotel."

"We know about the alignment tomorrow morning," Mallory said. "And the newel post's hidden compartment."

"Then you understand why people are dying," Gloria replied. "What's in that compartment could destroy the Harrington family and change who legally owns this hotel and everything in it."

"Do you know what's hidden there?" Tucker asked.

Gloria hesitated, then nodded. "Not exactly, but generally. Captain Harrington's journals, documenting his theft of Spanish artifacts from Miguel Rojas."

"Did Isabella Cruz discover this forty years ago?" Mallory pressed.

"Partial proof," Gloria said. "During the east wing renovations, she found a letter hidden in a wall cavity, a letter from Captain Harrington to his son, referencing the murder of Rojas and the hidden evidence. She brought it to me. She didn't know what to do."

"And what did you tell her?" Tucker asked gently.

Gloria's eyes filled with tears that she quickly blinked away. "I told her to return it, to speak with old Mr. Harrington—Vivian's father. I thought he would do the right thing." Her voice hardened. "I was wrong."

"Isabella was killed that night," Mallory said. It wasn't a question. It was a statement.

Gloria nodded. "She went to meet Mr. Harrington in his study. I never saw her alive again. The next morning, they found her body near the beach stairs."

"Did you tell the police?" Tucker asked.

"I tried," Gloria said bitterly. "The detective in charge was a family friend of the Harringtons. My statement about the letter and Isabella's meeting with Mr. Harrington was taken but never included in the official report. They ruled it a random attack by an intruder."

"And you've kept this secret for forty years," Mallory said. "Why?"

Gloria's expression was a complex mixture of shame and defiance. "I had three young children, including Diego. No husband, no other job prospects. The Harringtons offered to keep me on, to ensure my family was provided for. In return, I kept silent."

"Until recently," Tucker said. "When you helped Edwin Blackwood access the original case files."

"I'm an old woman now," Gloria said simply. "My children are grown, my career is nearly over. And the guilt of what happened to Isabella has weighed heavily on me every day for forty years. When Edwin started asking questions, showing me documents that proved what I'd always suspected about Captain Harrington and Miguel Rojas... I told myself it was time for the truth to come out."

"Did you tell your son about this?" Mallory asked. "Detective Santos?"

"Only recently," Gloria admitted. "When Edwin was killed, I knew the cycle was starting again. I couldn't let Diego investigate blindly, not understanding the forces involved."

"Do you know where Francisco Ruiz is?" Tucker asked. "He's missing, and we're concerned."

Gloria shook her head. "Francisco called in sick this morning. Said he wasn't feeling well after being out in the storm yesterday. But when I went to check on him at his cottage, he wasn't there. His truck is gone too."

"Could he have gone to a doctor?" Mallory asked.

"It's possible," Gloria said. "But Francisco hates doctors. Has for years. And he left no message about where he was going." Her expression grew more troubled. "I am worried about him."

"Do you think he's in danger?" Tucker asked.

"I think anyone who knows about the alignment and the Harrington family's secrets is in danger," Gloria replied grimly. "Edwin and Pierre are already dead. Francisco is missing. And I…" she glanced at the door, lowering her voice further, "I've received warnings. Nothing explicit, but notes left in my office. 'Keep your mouth shut.' That kind of thing."

"Have you told Detective Santos about these threats?" Mallory asked.

"No," Gloria admitted. "They started before Edwin's death, and I thought they were just… intimidation. Now I'm not so sure."

"Do you have any idea who might be behind them?" Tucker asked.

Gloria hesitated. "I've worked here a long time. I observe things. Relationships, behaviors, patterns. There are several people who might have motives to protect the Harrington secrets—or exploit them."

"Such as?" Mallory asked.

"Judge Kincaid has been researching salvage law as it relates to the Harrington collection for months," Gloria said. "His wife is an expert in Spanish colonial artifacts. Mr. Marsh represents a collector who has tried repeatedly to acquire items from the hotel's archives. And Ms. Winters... she's writing a book about maritime mysteries, including the Harrington connection to the 1715 fleet."

"And Vivian Harrington herself?" Tucker asked.

"Vivian is... complicated," Gloria replied carefully. "She presents herself as merely the current caretaker of the family legacy, but she's intensely protective of it. Whether that extends to murder..." She shrugged. "I couldn't say."

"What about the old cemetery on the property?" Mallory asked. "Ruiz mentioned it might be significant somehow."

Gloria nodded. "The original Harrington family plot. It's been abandoned since the 1920s when they began using the city cemetery instead. Captain James Harrington is buried there, along with his wife and eldest son. Francisco believes that's where the original cache was hidden, beneath the Captain's grave."

"But it was moved during renovations," Tucker said.

"According to hotel records, yes," Gloria said. "When they expanded the east wing in 1904, they did substantial foundation work near the cemetery. The cache was supposedly discovered and relocated within the hotel itself."

"To the newel post," Mallory said.

"That's what Edwin believed," Gloria replied. "Based on the architectural plans and Captain Harrington's journals. The alignment tomorrow will reveal if he was right."

The sound of a cart in the hallway alerted them to someone approaching. Gloria straightened, immediately resuming her professional demeanor.

"The southwest corner of the cemetery has the oldest graves," she said in a normal voice. "Including the Captain's."

With that, she opened the door and left, nodding to a house-keeper pushing a linen cart past the closet.

Tucker and Mallory waited a moment, then left as well, heading back toward their room to regroup.

"Southwest corner," Tucker murmured as they walked. "She was giving us directions."

"And a warning," Mallory said. "She seems genuinely concerned about Ruiz."

In their room, they quickly changed into more casual clothes suitable for exploring the grounds, including sturdy shoes that could handle the muddy conditions after the storm.

"If Ruiz is missing rather than just avoiding work, that's a significant development," Tucker said as they prepared.

"And he apparently knows something about the ceme-tery's connection to the treasure," Mallory said. "Which makes him dangerous to whoever is protecting these secrets."

"Or valuable to someone trying to find them," Tucker countered. "Ruiz could have been coerced into helping locate the original cache site."

They reached the lobby at two o'clock to find Cordelia Winters already waiting, dressed in practical pants and boots that seemed at odds with her usual dramatic style. She carried a small backpack and was wearing a wide-brimmed hat.

"Ready for our historical exploration?" she asked with a knowing look.

"Just a casual walk of the grounds," Tucker replied for the benefit of anyone who might be listening. "Taking advantage of the break in the weather."

They exited through the main doors and followed a flag-stone path that led through the formal gardens, deserted due to the damp conditions, which suited their purposes perfectly.

"Gloria Mendez mentioned the significance of the cemetery," Mallory said quietly as they walked. "Particularly the southwest corner, where Captain Harrington is buried."

As they left the manicured gardens behind, the path became less defined, winding through the trees and undergrowth where the landscape had been allowed to return to its natural state. After about five minutes of walking, they reached a low stone wall, partially crumbled in places that apparently marked the boundary of the old cemetery.

The burial ground was small by modern standards—perhaps forty feet square—and heavily overgrown. Ancient live oaks draped with Spanish moss created a cathedral-like canopy above weathered headstones tilting at various angles. Some had fallen completely, while others remained upright but were so eroded by time and weather that their inscriptions were barely legible.

"This way," Mallory said, heading toward the southwest corner. "Gloria mentioned this is where the oldest graves are located."

The southwest section was dominated by three larger monuments—a central obelisk flanked by two ornate headstones with angels carved into their tops. The obelisk bore the name "HARRINGTON" in large letters, with "Captain James Harrington, 1822-1889" below it.

"The family patriarch," Cordelia murmured. "Founder of the hotel and, if Edwin's research is correct, murderer of Miguel Rojas."

Tucker examined the grave markers carefully. "The bases are substantial. If something was hidden here, it would likely be beneath one of these larger monuments."

Mallory was already circling the captain's obelisk, studying its foundation. "Look at this," she called, pointing to one side of the base. "These marks don't match the weathering pattern of the rest of the stone. Almost like..."

"Someone has moved it recently," Tucker finished for her, crouching to examine the scratches in the stone and the disturbed earth around the base. "Within the last day or two, judging by how fresh these marks are."

"And look there," Cordelia said, pointing to a nearby tree. "Tire tracks. Someone drove close to the cemetery, despite the 'No Vehicles Beyond This Point' sign we passed earlier."

Tucker frowned, following the tracks with his eyes. "They lead in from that service road," he said, "directly to this corner of the cemetery, then back out again. It seems Captain Harrington has had recent visitors."

"Ruiz, d'you think?" Mallory said. "His truck is missing, too."

"Possibly," Tucker said. "But why would he damage a grave he's maintained for decades? Unless he was desperate to find something."

"Or someone made him show them where it was," Cordelia said grimly.

A thorough examination of the obelisk's base revealed a small cavity underneath it, accessed by shifting one section of the stone foundation. The space was empty, but showed signs of recent disturbance—the earth had been freshly turned.

"It looks to me as if something has been removed from here," Tucker said, standing up. "And recently."

"But what?" Mallory said. "If the main cache was relocated to the newel post in 1904, what could have been hidden here that someone would want after all this time?"

"A key, perhaps," Cordelia said. "Or documentation about the original cache. Something that would help access or authenticate what's hidden in the hotel."

Tucker's phone rang, interrupting their speculation. The screen showed Santos' number.

"Detective," Tucker answered, putting the call on speaker so Mallory and Cordelia could hear.

"We've found Francisco Ruiz," Santos said without preamble, his tone grave. "He's in the St. Augustine General Hospital. He was admitted last night with a concussion and multiple contusions. He was found unconscious in his truck at Fort Matanzas, about ten miles south of the hotel."

"Is he awake?" Tucker asked. "Has he said what happened?"

"He regained consciousness about an hour ago," Santos replied. "He claims he can't remember anything after leaving his cottage yesterday evening. The doctors believe it's temporary amnesia from the head trauma."

"Or he's afraid to say what he knows," Mallory said.

"That's my assessment," Santos said. "I'm posting an officer outside his room as a precaution. Where are you three right now?"

Tucker exchanged glances with Mallory and Cordelia, surprised that Santos knew they were together. "We're exploring the hotel grounds. How did you know Cordelia was with us?"

"Security cameras in the lobby," Santos explained. "And I have officers maintaining discreet surveillance of all guests connected to this investigation. Which is why I know you're currently in the old cemetery, examining Captain Harrington's grave."

Tucker couldn't help but be impressed by the detective's thoroughness. "So why did you ask?" he said.

"To see if you would answer truthfully," Santos replied.

Tucker slowly shook his head, then said, "We've found evidence that someone recently accessed a hidden compartment beneath the obelisk. Fresh tool marks on the stonework, disturbed earth, tire tracks leading to and from the site."

"Interesting timing," Santos said. "Ruiz was attacked last night, and the grave was disturbed around the same time. I think the two events are almost certainly connected."

"Whoever did this may have forced Ruiz to show them the compartment's location," Mallory said. "Then attacked him to shut him up."

"Or to prevent him from accessing something they wanted for themselves," Cordelia said. "If Ruiz knew about both hiding places—the grave and the newel post—he would be valuable to someone searching for the Harrington secrets."

"Either way, we now have two murders and possibly an attempted third," Santos said. "All connected to whatever is hidden in that hotel. I'm increasing security for tonight and tomorrow morning, but keeping it as unobtrusive as possible to avoid alerting our suspects."

"And we'll head back to the hotel," Tucker said.

After ending the call, they took one last look at the disturbed grave site. Whatever had been hidden there was long gone, taken by someone willing to commit violence to get it. And tomorrow morning, during the brief window of the celestial alignment, that same person would likely attempt to access the newel post's secret compartment.

12

MIDNIGHT ENCOUNTER

THE REST OF THE AFTERNOON PASSED IN A STATE OF heightened vigilance. After returning from the cemetery, Tucker and Mallory spent several hours reviewing Blackwood's files on the USB drive, searching for any details they might have missed about the alignment mechanism and what exactly was hidden in the newel post.

"I wonder why someone hasn't torn that newel post down and taken it apart," Mallory muttered.

"It's pretty substantial," Tucker replied. "Carved from a single piece of oak. To remove it would mean the destruction of the entire staircase, big job. And you can bet the family has protected it and what's in it, if anything," Tucker replied.

"According to these notes," Mallory said, scrolling through a document on her laptop, "Blackwood believed the post contains documentation of Captain Harrington's crimes and a map to where the actual artifacts are hidden."

"So the alignment reveals the secrets, but not the treasure itself," Tucker mused. "Interesting."

"The treasure must still be somewhere else on the property," Mallory said. "Or it might have been moved off-site decades ago."

"Either way, the documentation is the key," Tucker said. "Proof of theft and murder would invalidate the Harrington claim to whatever was salvaged from the 1715 fleet, regardless of where it's currently located."

"Which explains why someone is willing to kill to prevent that proof from being found," Mallory said grimly.

As evening approached, they ventured downstairs for dinner, carefully noting the presence and behavior of their primary suspects. Judge Kincaid and Elaine dined together. Their conversation appeared to be intense, but too distant to overhear. Gregory Marsh was once again alone, though he seemed more relaxed than he did at lunch, occasionally making notes on his phone between courses.

Vivian Harrington appeared briefly in the dining room, checking on operations and greeting guests, though the strain of the recent events showed in the tight lines around her eyes. She stopped briefly at their table.

"I trust you're still enjoying your stay," she said, her tone suggesting she recognized the absurdity of the statement given the circumstances.

"Yes, of course. The hotel and grounds are beautiful," Tucker replied diplomatically.

"Yes, well, the Harrington has weathered worse in its long history," Vivian said with a thin smile. "Tomorrow we'll begin returning to normalcy. Chef Dupont's assistant has agreed to step up as interim executive chef, and we've arranged a special breakfast service to compensate for the disruptions."

"Beginning at what time?" Mallory asked innocently.

"Service starts at eight, though the dining room opens at seven for coffee and pastries," Vivian replied. "Will you be joining us, or do you prefer room service?"

"We'll come down," Tucker said. "It's always nice to start the day with proper table service."

After Vivian moved on, Mallory leaned closer. "She didn't mention anything special about the event tomorrow morning," she murmured.

"Either she doesn't know about the alignment," Tucker replied quietly, "or she's being very careful not to draw attention to it."

Cordelia Winters entered the dining room late, pausing briefly at their table. "Detective Santos visited Ruiz at the hospital again," she informed them in a low voice. "He's still claiming memory loss, but the doctors say he's improving. I have contacts at the hospital—they're keeping me updated. I'll talk to you later, perhaps." And with that, she smiled, turned away and went to her table.

After dinner, they returned to their room, aware that the hotel seemed unusually quiet for a Friday evening. Many guests had departed following the murders, and those who remained appeared subdued, the usual vacation atmosphere replaced by something more cautious and watchful.

"We should get some sleep," Tucker said as they prepared for bed. "Tomorrow will be busy, especially around 10 AM."

"I'm not sure I can sleep," Mallory replied. "There are too many questions still unanswered. Who attacked Ruiz? What was taken from the cemetery? And why kill Blackwood and Dupont, but only attack Ruiz?"

"Different circumstances, perhaps," Tucker theorized. "Blackwood and Dupont were killed within the hotel, where the perpetrator could control the environment. Ruiz was attacked out of sight in the grounds, possibly in a hurry."

"Or by someone less experienced with violence," Mallory said. "Someone who couldn't bring themselves to commit outright murder."

They continued discussing theories as they settled in for

the night, finally turning out the lights around eleven. Despite her earlier claim, Mallory fell asleep quickly, the events of the past two days having taken their toll on her energy reserves.

Tucker, however, remained awake, his mind processing the various pieces of evidence and potential scenarios. His years in the FBI had trained him to recognize patterns in human behavior, to anticipate actions based on motivation and opportunity. Their killer had demonstrated both careful planning and adaptability: staging Blackwood's death to look like an accident, then taking advantage of the power outage to eliminate Dupont.

The attack on Ruiz was an escalation and perhaps an act of desperation as the alignment date approached. Tomorrow morning would be the culmination of whatever plan the perpetrator had set in motion. The question was, would they try to access the newel post during the alignment? Or had they already got what they needed from the cemetery?

Tucker's thoughts were interrupted by a soft sound from the hallway, not the usual noises of a hotel at night, but something more deliberate. He sat up, instantly alert, straining to identify the source.

There it was again, a subtle scratching, like someone testing their door lock.

Silently, Tucker rose from the bed, careful not to disturb Mallory. He moved to the door and peered through the peephole, but the hallway was dark.

Another power outage? Or something deliberately arranged?

The scratching sound stopped. Tucker waited, listening intently. Then came a new sound, soft footsteps moving away from their door, toward the stairwell rather than the elevators.

Tucker quickly pulled on pants and a shirt, slipped his

phone into his pocket, and eased the door open, looking both ways before stepping into the hallway. The emergency lights provided minimal illumination, casting long shadows that made identification difficult. At the far end of the corridor, a figure disappeared through the stairwell door.

Moving silently, Tucker followed, maintaining enough distance to avoid detection while keeping the figure in sight. The stairwell was even darker, forcing him to rely more on sound than sight as he tracked the intruder downward.

They bypassed the lobby level, continuing to the ground floor, where the figure exited the stairwell. Tucker waited a few seconds before following, emerging into a service corridor he hadn't seen before. He was in the hotel's maintenance area, normally off-limits to guests.

The corridor led past storage rooms, a laundry facility, and what appeared to be staff changing areas, before ending at a heavy door marked "Archives - Authorized Personnel Only." The figure had vanished, presumably through this door, which now stood slightly ajar.

Tucker approached cautiously, aware that he could be walking into a trap. He eased the door open further, revealing a large room lined with filing cabinets, bookshelves, and glass display cases. In the center, illuminated by the beam of a small flashlight, stood Elaine Kincaid, examining a folder of documents spread on a table.

She hadn't noticed him yet. Her attention was focused entirely on whatever she was reading. Tucker watched her for a moment, noting the methodical way she photographed each page with her phone before moving on to the next document.

"Finding anything interesting, Mrs. Kincaid?" he asked quietly, stepping into the room.

Elaine started violently, nearly dropping her phone. The

flashlight beam swung wildly before settling on Tucker's face.

"Mr. Randall," she said, her voice surprisingly steady despite her obvious surprise. "You startled me."

"That seems to be going around," Tucker replied mildly. "Especially when people are somewhere they shouldn't be, in the middle of the night, during another convenient power outage."

Elaine lowered the flashlight slightly, though not enough to completely remove him from its beam. "I could say the same about you. These archives are restricted."

"I followed someone who tried to break into my room," Tucker explained. "Someone who then came directly here. Care to explain why you were testing our door lock at midnight?"

"I wasn't at your room," Elaine snapped, though something flickered in her expression. Was it calculation rather than genuine outrage? "I came directly here from my suite. The judge is a sound sleeper, and I needed to verify some information for his book."

"At midnight? During a power outage? Without authorization?" Tucker's tone made it clear he didn't believe her.

Elaine sighed, setting down both the flashlight and her phone. "Alright, Mr. Randall. Cards on the table. I'm not breaking into rooms or committing murders, if that's what you're implying. I'm conducting research that Vivian Harrington would prefer remained buried."

"Research into Captain Harrington's theft of Spanish artifacts," Tucker said, watching her reaction.

If she was surprised by his knowledge, she hid it well. "Among other things. Walter's book focuses on how wealthy families have used legal maneuvering to protect questionable assets. The Harringtons are a perfect case study; a fortune built on stolen salvage, protected through generations by strategic donations to law enforcement, judges, and politicians."

"And your interest in this? Beyond supporting your husband's work?" Tucker pressed.

"Professional curiosity," Elaine replied. "Before I married Walter, I worked with Harrison Blackwood, Edwin's uncle. We spent years researching the 1715 fleet, and those who salvaged it. Harrison was convinced the Harringtons possessed artifacts that rightfully belonged to Miguel Rojas's descendants."

"Descendants who would have legal claim if proof of theft could be established," Tucker said.

"Exactly," Elaine said, nodding. "And that proof supposedly exists in documents hidden somewhere in this hotel, documents that will be accessible tomorrow morning during the alignment."

"Documents Edwin Blackwood was close to finding before he was murdered," Tucker said pointedly.

Elaine met his gaze steadily. "Yes. Edwin continued his uncle's work after he died. We stayed in touch over the years, comparing notes. He contacted me three days before his death, said he'd found something significant, proof of Captain Harrington's crimes hidden in the hotel's architecture."

"And now you're searching the archives for confirmation," Tucker said. "But why try to access our room?"

Elaine hesitated, then seemed to reach a decision. "Because Edwin mentioned leaving key evidence in a safe deposit box, accessible through a series of clues. When I saw you and your wife return from town yesterday morning, then later overheard you discussing documents you'd retrieved, I thought perhaps…"

"You thought we had found what Edwin had hidden," Tucker finished for her. "But breaking into our room is a serious crime, Mrs. Kincaid. As is attacking Francisco Ruiz."

"I had nothing to do with that," Elaine said firmly. "Nor with Edwin's murder or Chef Dupont's. Yes, I've been conducting unauthorized research, but I'm not a killer. I'm trying to establish historical truth and legal ownership, something Walter and I have dedicated our careers to."

Tucker studied her, assessing her sincerity, and decided that while Elaine was clearly holding something back, her denial of any involvement in the violence seemed genuine.

"What do you know about the compartment beneath Captain Harrington's grave?" he asked.

Surprise flickered across her face. "The cemetery? I wasn't aware of anything hidden there. My research has focused on the newel post and the alignment mechanism."

"Someone accessed a hidden space beneath the obelisk last night," Tucker informed her. "The same night Ruiz was attacked. Where were you last night, Mrs. Kincaid?"

"I was with Walter all last evening," Elaine replied. "We dined in our room, then watched a movie. The hotel staff can confirm our room service order, and Walter is hardly the type to attack an elderly gardener."

Before Tucker could respond, the lights suddenly came back on, flooding the archives with brightness. They both blinked against the sudden illumination.

"I should go," Elaine said, quickly gathering the documents she'd been examining. "Walter will wonder where I am if he wakes."

"We're not finished discussing this," Tucker said. "Whatever you're looking for, two people have already died because of it, and a third nearly joined them. This isn't just academic research anymore."

"I understand the seriousness," Elaine assured him, returning the folder to a filing cabinet. "But I'm not your killer, Mr. Randall. Perhaps we should compare notes instead of treating each other as suspects. After all, we both seem to be pursuing the same truth."

"We can discuss it tomorrow," Tucker said. "After we see what the alignment reveals."

"If someone doesn't prevent that revelation from happening," Elaine replied grimly. "Whoever killed Edwin and Pierre won't stop now, not when they're so close to either securing or destroying the evidence."

As they prepared to leave the archives, Tucker couldn't shake the feeling that Elaine was still withholding significant information. Whether that made her a suspect or merely a competitor in the race to uncover the Harrington secrets remained to be seen.

What was certain was that tomorrow morning's alignment would bring matters to a head, one way or another.

13

HIGH TIDE REVELATIONS

TUCKER RETURNED TO THEIR ROOM TO FIND MALLORY AWAKE and more than a little concerned.

"Where have you been?" she demanded, visibly relieved. "I woke up, and you were gone. The power was out, and after what happened to Blackwood and Dupont..."

"I'm sorry," Tucker apologized, closing and locking the door behind him. "Elaine Kincaid tried to break into our room. I followed her."

Mallory's eyes widened. "What?"

Tucker quickly recounted his midnight encounter in the archives. "She claims she was just conducting research for the judge's book, but she admitted trying to break in here, thinking we might have evidence Edwin left behind."

"Do you believe her?" Mallory asked, sitting on the edge of the bed.

Tucker considered the question. "Eh... Some of it. I think she's genuinely interested in the legal implications of proving the Harrington fortune was built on theft and murder. But I think she's hiding something."

"Such as her connection to Harrison Blackwood?"

Mallory said. "Cordelia mentioned they worked together before she married the judge."

"That part she admitted," Tucker said. "But she denied any knowledge of the cemetery hiding place or involvement in attacking Ruiz."

"So, who did attack him?" Mallory said, frowning. "And what was taken from beneath the grave?"

Tucker shook his head. "I don't know. But Elaine made a good point. Whoever t was that killed Blackwood and Dupont won't stop now, not when they're so close to either securing or destroying the evidence."

"And the alignment is in less than ten hours," Mallory said, checking the clock. "We should try to get some sleep. Tomorrow will be crucial."

Despite the lingering questions, they managed a few hours of rest before dawn broke, revealing a clear sky for the first time since they'd arrived at the Harrington. The storm had finally passed, leaving behind crisp, cool air and perfect visibility, ideal conditions for the celestial alignment.

They dressed, opting for casual clothing that wouldn't draw attention but still allowed freedom of movement if necessary. Tucker secured the brass key from the safe deposit box in his pocket, ensuring it was easily accessible when and if it was needed.

"Remember," he said as they prepared to head downstairs, "we stay together at all times. Santos has officers in the hotel, but they can't protect us if we separate."

"Agreed," Mallory nodded. "And we keep all our suspects in sight, especially as we approach alignment time."

The dining room was busier than expected when they arrived for breakfast. Despite the reduced guest count following the murders, those who remained seemed determined to maintain normal routines. Gregory Marsh was at his usual table by the windows, the Kincaids in a corner engaged in quiet conversation, and Cordelia Winters was just being seated near the entrance.

"Strategic positioning," Mallory murmured as they were shown to a table with a clear view of both the dining room and the lobby beyond. "Everyone wants to observe without being obvious about it."

Tucker nodded, scanning for Detective Santos or his officers. He spotted one plainclothes detective near the buffet table and another positioned in the lobby, both maintaining casual poses while clearly monitoring the hotel guests.

They ordered breakfast and ate slowly, more focused on their surroundings than the food. As they finished, Santos himself entered the dining room, nodding slightly in their direction before taking a seat at the bar where he could observe the entire space.

"It's nearly nine," Mallory said, checking her watch. "We should position ourselves near the staircase before others get the same idea."

They exited the dining room and moved to a seating area in the lobby with a clear view of the grand staircase and its ornate newel post. The morning sunlight streamed through the hotel's front windows, not yet at the angle that would create the crucial shadow pattern, but steadily advancing toward it.

Mallory opened a guidebook to St. Augustine's historic sites, the perfect prop for two tourists relaxing in a hotel lobby. Behind its cover, she murmured, "Elaine keeps checking her watch. Judge Kincaid seems tense. And Marsh has positioned himself near that display case with a direct line of sight to the newel post."

"Cordelia just entered the lobby," Tucker said quietly. "She's heading for the front desk, but keeping an eye on the staircase."

"And Vivian's in her office," Mallory said, gesturing subtly toward the partially open door behind the reception desk. "Perfect view of the main staircase from her desk."

As the minutes ticked by, the lobby grew busier with guests checking out or planning their day's activities. Most passed through quickly, but Tucker noticed a gradual increase in people who seemed to find reasons to linger— checking phones, consulting maps, or simply resting on the various couches and chairs scattered throughout the space.

By 9:45, the casual observer might not have noticed anything unusual, but to Tucker's trained eye, it was a tableau of multiple parties positioning themselves for the coming alignment, all trying to appear nonchalant while maintaining optimal vantage points.

"Detective Santos is moving closer to the staircase," Mallory whispered. "And I just spotted Gloria near the service entrance. Everyone's converging."

At 10:00, Tucker observed a subtle shift in the quality of light entering through the front windows. The sun had reached an angle where its rays were beginning to create distinct patterns on the lobby floor.

"Twelve minutes," he murmured to Mallory. "Let's move closer. We need to be within reach of the newel post when the alignment occurs."

They rose casually, as if preparing to head out for the day, and strolled toward the grand staircase. But others, so it seemed, had the same idea. Gregory Marsh was now exam- ining a historical photograph on the wall beside the stairs, while Elaine Kincaid had positioned herself on the bottom step, apparently waiting for her husband, who was speaking with the concierge.

At 10:05, Santos received a call on his phone, his expres- sion changing as he listened to whatever was being said. Then, after a brief conversation, he hurried to the front entrance and disappeared outside.

"That's not good," Tucker murmured. "Something's pulled him away at the critical moment."

"A deliberate distraction, d'you think?" Mallory said quietly.

"Possibly," Tucker said. "Stay alert."

At 10:10, the lobby fell into an almost unnatural hush. Even guests not aware of the coming alignment seemed to sense the tension in the air, conversations became whispers or ceased all together. All eyes—whether openly or covertly—were fixed on the grand staircase and the great, ornate newel post at its base.

The sunlight streaming through the front windows had narrowed to a specific beam that was steadily advancing across the lobby floor toward the staircase. Tucker positioned himself against the wall near the newel post with Mallory at his side, both maintaining casual postures while remaining ready to act.

At precisely 10:12, the beam of light struck a decorative glass element in one of the windows, refracting into a perfect line that speared across the lobby and illuminated the newel post. As the light touched the carved wooden column, something remarkable happened—shadow patterns formed by the post's intricate carvings resolved into a distinct design on the lobby floor.

"A keyhole," Mallory breathed, low enough that only Tucker could hear. "Just like Blackwood's diagrams showed."

But the answer wasn't cast on the floor as they'd expected. Instead, the shadow was projected onto the rounded cap of the newel post itself, revealing a pattern invisible under normal lighting conditions—a small keyhole disguised within the carved ship motif.

Tucker reached into his pocket for the brass key as movement erupted around them. Gregory Marsh pushed forward from his position by the wall, while Elaine Kincaid rose from the bottom step. From her office, Vivian Harrington emerged with surprising speed.

"Now," Tucker murmured to Mallory, who smoothly interposed herself between Tucker and the advancing Marsh, appearing to accidentally bump into him while apologizing profusely.

The distraction gave Tucker the seconds he needed. He inserted the brass key into the shadow-revealed keyhole and turned it smoothly. A soft click was barely audible amid the growing commotion as a hidden mechanism activated within the newel post.

The rounded cap rotated slightly, then lifted to reveal a small compartment within the post itself. Tucker reached in quickly, extracting a leather pouch before anyone else could interfere.

"Police! Everyone stay where you are!"

Detective Santos' voice cut through the lobby as he re-entered through the front doors, flanked by two uniformed officers. He moved directly to Tucker's side, positioning himself between the gathered suspects and the item Tucker had retrieved.

"Please step back," Santos instructed the onlookers firmly. "This is now an active crime scene investigation."

The lobby erupted in confused murmurs as hotel guests not involved in the treasure hunt tried to understand what was happening. Vivian Harrington stepped forward, her composure maintained through obvious effort.

"Detective, what is the meaning of this?" she demanded. "These are hotel guests, not criminals."

"That remains to be determined," Santos replied evenly. "Mr. Randall, please hand me the item you just retrieved."

Tucker complied, passing the leather pouch to Santos, who examined it briefly before securing it in an evidence bag.

"I need everyone to remain in the lobby," Santos announced, addressing the gathered suspects. "Officers will take your statements individually. Mr. and Mrs. Randall, please come with me."

As Santos led them toward Vivian's office, Tucker caught glimpses of the other suspects' reactions. Gregory Marsh's barely concealed frustration, Elaine Kincaid's calculating gaze, Judge Kincaid's stony expression, and Cordelia Winters' intense curiosity. Vivian herself followed them, her authority temporarily superseded by Santos' investigation.

Once the office door closed behind them, Santos placed the evidence bag on Vivian's desk. "Now, let's see what was worth killing two people over."

"Three attempted murders," Tucker corrected. "Don't forget Ruiz."

"Who regained consciousness fully this morning," Santos informed them. "And has quite a story to tell."

"He remembers what happened?" Mallory asked eagerly.

Santos nodded. "Gregory Marsh approached him yesterday afternoon, asking about the old cemetery. When Ruiz refused to discuss it, Marsh offered a substantial bribe. Later that evening, Marsh returned with two men who forced Ruiz to take them to the Captain's grave and show them the hidden compartment beneath the obelisk."

"What did they take?" Tucker asked.

"According to Ruiz, a small metal box containing several old coins and a folded document," Santos replied. "After retrieving these items, the men attacked Ruiz, loaded him into his own truck, and abandoned him at Fort Matanzas. He regained consciousness briefly during the drive but pretended to remain unconscious to avoid further violence."

"And he's certain it was Marsh?" Mallory said.

"Positive," Santos affirmed. "We're arresting Marsh as we speak. His room has already been searched, revealing the coins and document taken from the cemetery, along with evidence connecting him to both murders."

"What kind of evidence?" Tucker asked.

"Chef Dupont's personal notebook, containing his observations about Edwin's research," Santos explained. "And traces of the same distinctive rope fibers found on Blackwood's body. It appears Marsh used similar techniques in both killings."

"That matches our timeline," Tucker said. "Marsh was absent during the power outage when Dupont was killed, and he had ample opportunity to catch Blackwood alone on the beach."

"But what was his motive?" Mallory asked. "Just the treasure? Or something more?"

"That's where this comes in," Santos said, carefully opening the leather pouch. Inside was a folded packet of papers, yellowed with age but surprisingly well-preserved, along with a small brass key different from the one they had used to open the newel post.

Santos gently unfolded the papers, revealing handwritten text in faded ink. "Captain James Harrington's confession," he announced after scanning the first page. "Detailing his murder of Miguel Rojas and theft of Spanish artifacts recovered from the 1715 fleet."

"The documentation Edwin was searching for," Mallory said.

"And this appears to be a detailed inventory of the stolen items," Santos continued, examining another page, "along with a map showing their hiding place. It's not in the hotel at all, but in a cave system along the coast, accessible only during specific tide conditions."

"High tide revelations," Tucker murmured, understanding the chapter title from Blackwood's research notes. "The treasure can only be reached when the tide reveals an underwater passage."

"Which explains the brass key," Santos said, indicating the second key from the leather pouch. "According to this note, it opens a waterproof chest hidden within the cave."

Vivian, who had been listening outside during this exchange, pushed the door open and stepped inside. "I knew nothing of this," she said, her voice uncharacteristically subdued. "My father never mentioned a confession, or murder, or stolen artifacts. I always believed our family's wealth came from legitimate salvage operations."

Santos studied her for a moment, assessing her sincerity. "Your father may not have known either. According to these documents, Captain Harrington created this hidden compartment specifically to preserve the truth for future generations, separate from the family's public history. The alignment mechanism ensured it would only be discovered by someone with both knowledge of the celestial pattern and the key to access it."

"But how did Blackwood get the key?" Mallory wondered.

"From Harrison Blackwood's collection," Santos explained. "Edwin's uncle had acquired it years ago through an antiquities dealer, not realizing its significance until he began researching the Harrington connection to the 1715 fleet. After Harrison's death, Edwin inherited the key along with his uncle's research notes."

"And Marsh knew about this through his connection to the antiquities market," Tucker surmised. "Perhaps he even represented the same collector who originally sold the key to Harrison Blackwood."

"Exactly," Santos said. "Marsh works for a wealthy client obsessed with the 1715 fleet. When he learned Edwin had discovered the alignment mechanism and possessed the key, he saw an opportunity to eliminate the competition and claim both the confession and the treasure map for his client."

"So he killed Blackwood before he could access the newel post," Mallory said. "Then Dupont when he realized the chef had knowledge of Edwin's research."

"And he attacked Ruiz to get whatever was hidden in the cemetery," Tucker said. "But what was the connection between the two hiding places? Why split the items?"

Santos consulted the documents again. "According to this note, Captain Harrington created redundancy in his system. The cemetery contained verification items: Spanish coins from the actual salvage and a letter from Rojas written shortly before his murder. Proof that would authenticate the confession hidden in the newel post."

"A failsafe," Tucker said, nodding. "Ensuring that even if one cache was discovered, it wouldn't make sense without the other."

"But why create this... such an elaborate system at all?" Mallory asked. "Why not simply destroy the evidence of his crimes?"

"Apparently, the Captain was dying when he created all this," Santos explained, indicating a passage in the confession. "He was riddled with guilt over Rojas's murder but unwilling to tarnish his family's reputation during his lifetime. This was his compromise: the truth preserved but hidden, to be revealed when the family could no longer be directly harmed by it."

"And now it has been," Vivian whispered. "After all these years."

Santos gathered the documents carefully. "These will need to be authenticated, of course. But if genuine, they could have significant legal implications regarding ownership of any artifacts recovered from Rojas's original salvage site."

"The cave location," Tucker said. "Have you identified it?"

"Not precisely," Santos admitted. "The coordinates provided are approximate by modern standards. And according to the tide tables, the next viable access window isn't for another three days."

"Plenty of time to organize a proper recovery operation," Mallory said.

"With appropriate archaeological oversight," Santos said. "These artifacts, if they still exist, represent significant historical value beyond their monetary worth."

A knock at the office door interrupted their discussion. One of Santos' officers entered, looking grim.

"Detective, we have a situation," he reported. "Gregory Marsh is gone. He slipped out during the commotion in the lobby. And he's taken a hostage. Gloria Mendez."

"What?" Santos snapped. "How the—?"

"He must have suspected we were closing in," the officer explained. "Witnesses saw him force Ms. Mendez into a service exit at gunpoint. They're likely heading for a vehicle."

"Or the beach access," Tucker said quickly. "If Marsh has the map from the cemetery, he might be trying to reach the cave during the current tide cycle."

Santos was already moving. "I need officers at all exits and beach access points. Alert the Coast Guard and marine patrol. If he's heading for the cave, he'll need a boat."

"We're coming with you," Tucker said.

Santos hesitated only briefly. "Fine, but you follow my lead. This man has already killed twice and won't hesitate to do so again."

As they hurried from the office, Vivian called after them, "The hotel maintains a small motorboat at our private dock. For guest excursions. It's kept fueled and ready."

Santos acknowledged this with a nod as they rushed through the lobby. The other suspects were being interviewed by officers. Judge Kincaid appearing particularly agitated as he demanded information about his wife, who was noticeably absent from the gathering.

"Elaine Kincaid is missing too," Tucker realized. "Could she be working with Marsh?"

"Or following him independently," Mallory said. "Remember, she worked with Harrison Blackwood. She could have figured out the cave location on her own."

They exited the hotel through the main doors, Santos rapidly directing his officers via radio as they hurried toward the beach access staircase. The tide was high, waves crashing against the base of the bluff where the wooden steps descended to the beach.

At the bottom, they scanned the shoreline in both directions. To the north, the beach curved gently southward with no sign of activity. But to the south, near the tide pools where Blackwood's body had been found, Tucker spotted movement—three figures making their way along the narrow strip of sand still exposed at high tide.

"There!" he pointed. "Marsh, Gloria, and that looks like Elaine with them."

Santos raised binoculars to confirm. "You're right. Marsh is armed, and he has Gloria by the arm. Elaine Kincaid appears to be following willingly." He grabbed his radio. "All units converge on south beach access point. Suspects heading toward the tide pools with a hostage. Marine units approach from seaward side with caution."

As they hurried along the beach, carefully maintaining distance to avoid alerting Marsh, Tucker noticed how the three figures ahead were navigating the increasingly difficult terrain. The high tide had left only a narrow passage between the water and the bluff, forcing them to climb over the rocky outcroppings.

"They're heading for that headland," Mallory said,

pointing to where the coastline jutted out about half a mile ahead. "The cave entrance must be there."

Santos coordinated with approaching officers via radio, organizing a careful convergence that wouldn't spook Marsh into harming his hostage. "We need to contain him before he reaches the cave system," he explained. "Once they're inside, the situation becomes exponentially more dangerous."

As they drew closer, they could see that Gloria appeared to be struggling, her movements hampered by age and fear but still resisting Marsh. Elaine followed closely behind, carrying what looked like diving equipment—clear evidence of their intention to access the underwater passage.

The race to reach the cave before Marsh could disappear into its depths lent urgency to their pursuit. Whatever treasure lay hidden within it wasn't worth another life today. And Tucker could only hope they could convince Marsh of that before it was too late.

14

THE THIRD DEATH

THE PURSUIT ALONG THE BEACH BECAME INCREASINGLY treacherous as the tide continued to rise, waves now crashing against the bluff in places, forcing Tucker, Mallory, and Santos to time their movements carefully to avoid being swept away. Ahead, Marsh and his captives faced the same challenges, their progress slowed by Gloria's resistance and the difficult terrain.

"He won't make it to the cave entrance in time," Santos said, checking his watch. "According to these tide tables, high tide peaks in less than fifteen minutes. After that, the water will begin receding."

"Unless that's exactly what he's counting on," Tucker said. "If the entrance is underwater at peak high tide, the receding water would gradually reveal it, making access easier but still requiring specialized equipment."

"Which explains the diving gear Elaine is carrying," Mallory said.

They'd closed to within a hundred yards of their quarry when Marsh suddenly stopped, turning to scan the beach behind him. He spotted them immediately, yanked Gloria closer and produced a pistol.

Santos raised his hand, signaling the officers spread back along the beach to halt. "We need to establish communication," he said, removing his radio from his belt. After a brief exchange with headquarters, he nodded. "Marsh's cell is still active. We're calling him now."

Moments later, they could see Marsh reach into his pocket with his free hand, keeping the gun visible as he answered his phone. Santos took the call on his own device, switching to the speaker so Tucker and Mallory could hear.

"This is Detective Santos, Mr. Marsh. You're surrounded. Release Ms. Mendez and surrender yourself."

"Not happening, Detective," Marsh's voice came through clearly despite the crashing waves. "I've invested too much to walk away now. The treasure in that cave is worth millions— legitimate salvage untouched for three centuries."

"Legitimate?" Santos challenged. "We've found Captain Harrington's confession. We know he murdered Miguel Rojas and stole his discovery. Any artifacts in that cave are stolen property."

A laugh carried through both the phone and the distance between them. "Ancient history, Detective. Statute of limitations expired centuries ago. Maritime salvage law recognizes the finder's rights, not some tenuous connection to long-dead victims."

"Modern courts might disagree," Santos countered. "Especially with documented proof of the original theft. But that's a legal battle for another day. Right now, my concern is Ms. Mendez's safety."

"She's my insurance policy," Marsh replied coldly. "Once I've secured the artifacts, I'll release her. Until then, keep your distance."

During this exchange, Tucker noticed Elaine Kincaid moving subtly away from Marsh, edging toward the water's edge while his attention was focused on the conversation with Santos. Her intentions weren't clear; whether she was attempting to escape or positioning herself for some other purpose.

"Mr. Marsh," Santos continued, "you're already facing two murder charges for Edwin Blackwood and Pierre Dupont, plus attempted murder of Francisco Ruiz. Don't add a hostage situation to your problems."

"Blackwood was getting too close," Marsh admitted surprisingly. "He had everything: the key, knowledge of the alignment, access to the hotel archives. When he confronted me about my client's interest in the 1715 fleet, I knew he'd figured it out. He had to be eliminated."

"And Chef Dupont?" Santos asked, signaling to his officers to continue spreading out along the beach while keeping Marsh talking.

"Collateral damage," Marsh said dismissively. "He knew too much about Blackwood's research. The power outage provided perfect cover. I only regret not handling Ruiz more permanently."

Tucker recognized what Santos was doing, getting Marsh to incriminate himself, creating a record of his confessions while distracting him from his officers' movements.

"And what about Judge Kincaid?" Santos asked, introducing a new element that caught Tucker by surprise. "Was his death necessary, too?"

There was a moment of silence from Marsh's end. Even at this distance, they could see he was confused. "What are you talking about? The judge is fine. I saw him in the lobby less than an hour ago."

Santos exchanged a glance with Tucker and Mallory. "Judge Kincaid suffered a fatal heart attack in the hotel library twenty minutes ago. Medical examiner is calling it suspicious, possibly poison."

This was news to Tucker and Mallory, who hadn't heard anything about the judge's death. Whether Santos was bluffing to throw Marsh off balance or sharing actual information, the effect was immediate. Marsh turned toward Elaine, his expression visible even at a distance.

"What did you do?" he demanded.

Elaine stood straighter, dropping the diving equipment at her feet. "What was necessary." her voice carried faintly across the beach. "Walter had outlived his usefulness. Once he understood what the documents contained, he insisted on proper legal channels. Museums, courts, historical societies." She sneered.

The dynamics on the beach had shifted dramatically. What had appeared to be a hostage situation with Marsh controlling both women now revealed itself to be something much more complex: two killers with competing agendas, temporarily allied but fundamentally at odds.

Santos muted his phone briefly. "This changes things. Elaine's involvement complicates our approach."

"Judge Kincaid is actually dead?" Mallory asked quietly.

Santos nodded grimly. "He was found in the library with a torn page from an old hotel registry clutched in his hand."

"So both Marsh and Elaine are killers," Tucker said. "Working separately toward the same goal."

"With different endgames," Santos said, unmuting his phone. "Mr. Marsh, the situation has changed. You're now facing a potentially hostile accomplice, in addition to police intervention."

"We're not accomplices," Marsh spat into the phone. "This was supposed to be a simple recovery operation. The Kincaids inserted themselves. They complicated everything with their legal posturing."

"Yet you both ended up on this beach, headed for the same cave," Santos said. "That's quite a coincidence."

"It's no coincidence," Elaine called out, having moved further away from Marsh, clearly wanting to be heard. "My husband and Edwin were both pursuing the Harrington's secret from the legal angle, but I recognized the potential value of the artifacts. I knew Marsh was responsible for Edwin's death, and that he must have found something. Walter had all the pieces but lacked vision," Elaine continued. "He was more interested in legal precedent. I simply... refined the approach."

Marsh had grown visibly agitated during this exchange. His grip on Gloria tightened while his attention flipped back and forth between Elaine, Santos, and the police positioned along the beach. The tide had reached its peak. Waves were now lapping at their feet, making their position increasingly precarious.

"Enough talking," he shouted, waving his gun. "We're going to the cave entrance. Anyone follows, the old woman dies."

He ended the call, put his phone in his pocket, and began backing away, dragging Gloria with him while keeping the gun visible. Elaine hesitated, then quickly gathered the diving equipment and followed, apparently deciding her best chance still lay with Marsh despite their newly revealed antagonism.

"We need to end this before they reach the cave system," Santos muttered, signaling to his officers. "Once they're inside, we lose all tactical advantage."

Tucker, who had been studying the coastline, noted how the rising tide had changed the profile of the beach. "Look at that rock formation ahead of them," he pointed. "The water's creating a bottleneck. They'll have to wade through that section. That will slow them down."

"And giving us an opportunity to close the gap," Santos said, waving his officers forward.

They advanced carefully, maintaining enough distance to avoid provoking Marsh while ensuring they didn't lose sight of them. As predicted, when Marsh, Gloria, and Elaine reached the rocky bottleneck, they were forced to wade into thigh-deep water, and their progress slowed.

What happened next occurred with stunning speed. As Marsh negotiated the difficult passage, pulling Gloria alongside him, Elaine moved suddenly, swinging one of the oxygen tanks she'd been carrying. The metal cylinder connected with the back of Marsh's head, sending him stumbling forward into deeper water. His grip on Gloria loosened enough for the woman to break free, and she began wading toward the safety of the beach.

In the confusion, Marsh recovered his balance and turned on Elaine, raising his gun. But before he could fire, a wave caught him from behind, throwing him off balance. The shot went wide as Elaine lunged forward, both of them disappearing beneath the surging water between the rocks.

"Move in!" Santos shouted as Gloria made her way toward them and was quickly assisted by two officers who rushed forward to help her to safety.

Tucker and Mallory followed Santos to the water's edge, scanning the churning surf for signs of Marsh and Elaine. For several tense moments, nothing was visible but white foam and dark water swirling around the rocks. Then Elaine surfaced about twenty yards out, struggling against the current that threatened to sweep her further from shore.

Two officers rushed into the water, grabbed her, and dragged her to safety; there was still no sign of Marsh.

"Where is he?" Santos demanded as Elaine reached shallower water, coughing and sputtering.

"Underwater," she gasped. "His foot... caught between the rocks. Current too strong."

Santos immediately redirected his team, but the powerful

tide made approaching the spot where Marsh had disappeared extremely dangerous, and it quickly became clear they were fighting a lost cause: Marsh was gone.

As paramedics attended to Gloria and Elaine on the beach, Tucker and Mallory joined Santos at the water's edge.

"If Marsh is gone, that's three deaths connected to this case," Mallory said soberly.

"Four, counting Judge Kincaid," Santos corrected. "And all for what? Gold that's been sitting untouched in a cave for three centuries?"

A call from one of the dive team members drew Santos' attention. They had located Marsh's body, wedged between underwater rocks as Elaine had described. The tide had already turned, but recovery would have to wait for the water to recede further.

As they made their way back toward the hotel, Gloria Mendez walking slowly between two officers, Tucker reflected on the case's bizarre turn of events. Isabella Cruz had died in February 1985 after discovering part of the Harrington secret. Forty years later, almost to the day, four more people had died as that secret finally emerged from the shadows of history.

But unlike Isabella Cruz, whose murder had remained unsolved for forty years, the deaths of Blackwood, Chef Dupont, and Judge Kincaid would see justice. Elaine Kincaid was in custody, the evidence against her substantial, and the confession hidden by Captain Harrington in the newel post had finally served its purpose, bringing the truth to light after generations of concealment.

As they reached the wooden stairs leading back up to the hotel grounds, Tucker took Mallory's hand and squeezed it. Their honeymoon had turned into something neither of them had expected.

15

THE FEBRUARY ALIGNMENT

THE HARRINGTON HOTEL HAD BECOME A CRIME SCENE, ITS elegant lobby now strung with police tape as forensic technicians carefully documented the newel post mechanism and the surrounding area. Hotel guests had been relocated to other properties in St. Augustine. Only a skeleton staff remained, along with the investigators still piecing together all the aspects of the complex case.

In a conference room temporarily repurposed as an incident command center, Tucker and Mallory sat with Detective Santos, reviewing the events of the past few days. The documents recovered from the newel post were spread across the table, now protected in clear evidence sleeves.

"Captain Harrington's confession is remarkably detailed," Santos said, indicating the yellowed pages. "He documents not just Rojas's murder but the systematic campaign to discredit anyone who questioned his salvage claims."

"A conspiracy spanning decades," Tucker said. "With local officials, judges, even law enforcement involved in the cover-up."

"Which explains why Isabella Cruz's murder was never

properly investigated," Mallory said. "The Harrington influ-ence extended to the police department even forty years ago."

Santos nodded grimly. "My mother said as much. The detective who handled Cruz's case was a frequent guest at Harrington family events. The corruption wasn't even subtle. It was just the way things worked."

"And they continued to work until Edwin Blackwood started asking questions," Tucker said.

"For which he paid with his life," Santos said. "Along with Chef Dupont and Judge Kincaid."

"What about Elaine Kincaid?" Mallory asked. "Has she confessed to killing her husband?"

"Not explicitly," Santos replied. "But we all heard her, and the evidence is substantial. Traces of digitalis were found in her personal items, and more were found in his afternoon tea, which Elaine prepared personally. She's insisting that Marsh was responsible for all three deaths, but her story has multiple inconsistencies."

"And Marsh?" Tucker asked. "Has his body been recovered?"

"They retrieved his body during the afternoon low tide," Santos said. "Cause of death was drowning, but with signifi-cant contributing trauma to the back of the skull, consistent with being struck by an oxygen tank, as we saw, though Elaine insists it was self-defense rather than a calculated attack."

"What about the cave and its contents?" Mallory asked.

"That's become a complex jurisdictional issue," Santos explained. "The State Archaeological Division has taken control of the site, with federal authorities also involved because of maritime salvage implications. Initial exploration has confirmed the presence of artifacts: gold coins, jewelry, navigational instruments, and Timucua grave goods, all consistent with the 1715 fleet."

"And ownership?" Tucker pressed.

"That's where it gets complicated," Santos said, reaching for another file. "Captain Harrington's confession includes documentation of Miguel Rojas's original salvage claim, which was legally filed before his murder. Our researchers have located descendants of the Rojas family living in Miami. They'll have a legitimate claim to at least a portion of the value of the recovered artifacts."

"While the Harringtons lose not only the treasure but their historical legacy," Mallory said.

"Vivian has been cooperative throughout," Santos said. "She seems genuinely shocked by the revelations about her family's past. She's already announced her intention to establish a foundation dedicated to historical research and restitution, funded by the hotel's profits."

"A gesture of atonement," Tucker said. "Though it can't undo centuries of wrongdoing."

"Or bring back the dead," Mallory whispered.

They fell silent for a moment, contemplating the human cost of the Harrington secret—from Miguel Rojas in the 1880s to Judge Kincaid just days ago. Lives had ended prematurely to protect wealth built on deception and murder.

"What about Cordelia Winters?" Tucker asked, eventually. "What was her role in all this?"

"Primarily what she claimed," Santos replied. "She's a writer researching a historical mystery. She had connections to both Harrison Blackwood and Elaine from their previous work together, which is how she knew about the alignment theory. But she appears to have been pursuing literary inspiration rather than the actual treasure."

"She certainly has material for her next novel now," Mallory commented.

"Speaking of which," Santos said, "she left something for you." He retrieved an envelope from his briefcase and handed it to Tucker. "Said it was a token of her appreciation for your investigative help."

Tucker opened the envelope to find a brief note and a check for a substantial amount. "She's offering us an advance for the rights to our perspective on the case," he explained to Mallory after scanning the message. "For her next book."

"How generous," Mallory said with a small smile. "Though I'm not sure a murder-filled honeymoon is what most couples want to memorialize."

"It's certainly unique to us," Tucker acknowledged, returning her smile. "And somehow fitting, don't you think?"

Mallory smiled and slowly shook her head but didn't reply.

Santos gathered the evidence files, returning them to their designated storage containers. "The State Attorney will be filing formal charges against Elaine Kincaid tomorrow. With the evidence we've accumulated, conviction seems inevitable, despite her attempts to shift blame to Marsh."

"And Gloria Mendez?" Mallory asked. "How is she doing after her ordeal?"

"Remarkably well," Santos replied. "She's staying with my family while she recovers. After forty years of carrying the guilt of Isabella's death, she says she finally feels unburdened."

"And Francisco Ruiz?"

"Released from the hospital this morning," Santos said. "His testimony will be crucial in establishing the timeline of Marsh's activities and the attack at the cemetery. But physically, he's recovering well."

A knock at the conference room door interrupted their

conversation. An officer entered, handing Santos a folder of photographs. "The forensics team just delivered these, sir. Thought you'd want to see them immediately."

Santos examined the photographs with interest, then passed them to Tucker and Mallory. "These were taken during low tide this afternoon, when the cave entrance was fully exposed. The archaeologists were able to access the main chamber where the artifacts were stored."

The images showed a remarkable scene, a natural cave whose entrance was indeed underwater during high tide but fully accessible when the water receded. Inside, partially buried in sand but remarkably preserved, were wooden chests bound with metal, their contents partially visible in subsequent photos: gold coins, silver plates, jewelry set with gems that still caught the light despite centuries underwater.

"Amazing preservation," Tucker said. "The cave's unique tidal pattern must have created a protective environment, keeping the artifacts from degrading despite the saltwater exposure."

"The archaeological team is calling it one of the most significant finds related to the 1715 fleet," Santos said. "Both for its historical value and the intact nature of the collection."

"And all hidden in plain sight for centuries," Mallory marveled. "Just waiting for the right alignment of circumstances to be revealed."

"And the hidden newel post mechanism," Tucker said. "Its revelation is dependent on a specific celestial alignment that occurs only once every forty years. Captain Harrington was certainly thorough in his security measures."

"Fear of discovery is a powerful motivator," Santos said. "Preserving his secret became his life's work, even as guilt apparently drove him to create the mechanism that would eventually reveal his confession revelation."

"What a twisted mind, " Mallory said. "And what a contradiction, his wanting both concealment and disclosure."

"Human nature often is contradictory," Tucker replied. "Especially when faced with mortality. The Captain knew he was dying when he created these hiding places. He wanted to protect his family, but also perhaps his soul."

Santos began packing up the remaining files. "The case will continue unfolding for months," he said, "considering the archaeological recovery, the legal proceedings against Elaine Kincaid, and the ownership claims for the artifacts. But the immediate danger is past."

"Which means we can finally continue our honeymoon," Mallory said, looking at Tucker with raised eyebrows.

"Though perhaps at a different location," Tucker said with a smile. "Somewhere with fewer historical mysteries and murder plots."

"I hear the Caribbean is nice this time of year," Santos offered. "And remarkably free of century-old conspiracies."

"That sounds perfect," Mallory said, rising from her chair. "Sun, sand, and not a single alignment to worry about."

They thanked Santos for his cooperation throughout the investigation, promising to return if needed for Elaine's trial. As they left the conference room, the grand staircase caught Tucker's eye. Its newel post now marked with evidence tags but still elegant in its craftsmanship, but no longer hiding its secrets.

"It's remarkable to think how many people touched that post over the decades," he commented as they crossed the lobby. "Never knowing what was hidden inside."

"Like so many secrets," Mallory replied thoughtfully. "Visible only when the light hits them just right."

Outside, the February sun had begun its descent toward the horizon, casting long shadows across the hotel grounds. In the distance, they could see technicians still working at the beach access points, documenting the path Marsh and Elaine had taken in their final confrontation.

"I can't help but feel sorry for Vivian Harrington," Mallory said. "She seems to have taken it all rather well."

"I don't think she had much choice," Tucker replied. "And what about us? Our first case as husband and wife, rather than just professional partners."

"And we survived it," Mallory said with a smile. "In fact, I'd say we thrived under pressure. If we can handle multiple murders during our honeymoon, married life should be relatively straightforward."

Tucker laughed, taking her hand as they walked toward their rental car. "I wouldn't go that far. But I am looking forward to whatever comes next... as long as we face it together."

"Partners in all things," Mallory said, squeezing his hand. "Though I'm still voting for that Caribbean beach for our next adventure. Sun, sand, and absolutely no historical mysteries requiring investigation."

"Deal," Tucker said. "Two weeks of nothing more challenging than deciding which restaurant to try for dinner."

As they reached their car, Tucker paused for one last look at the Harrington Hotel, its Victorian elegance still imposing against the darkening sky.

"Ready?" Mallory asked, following his gaze to the hotel.

Tucker nodded, turning away. "More than ready."

It was over... or was it?

16

THE INTRUDER

THREE DAYS AFTER THE CONCLUSION OF THE DRAMATIC EVENTS at the Harrington Hotel, Tucker and Mallory had relocated to a small beachfront cottage about twenty miles south of St. Augustine. While it lacked the historic grandeur of the Harrington, the simple white bungalow offered privacy, tranquility, and—most importantly—no connection to centuries-old murder conspiracies. The perfect place to salvage what remained of their honeymoon.

They had spent the day on the beach, enjoying the simple pleasures: swimming, reading, walking hand-in-hand along the shore and, well, you know. As evening approached, they were seated together on the cottage's small deck, watching the waves surge back and forth and the darkening horizon.

"This is more like it," Mallory sighed contentedly, sipping a glass of wine. "No murders to solve, no killers to track, no historical mysteries demanding our attention."

"Just us," Tucker said, "and absolute peace and quiet."

Their peaceful moment was interrupted by the chime of Tucker's phone. He checked the screen, raising an eyebrow at the caller ID.

"Detective Santos," he muttered before answering. "Detective, how are things progressing in St. Augustine?"

He listened for a few moments, his expression growing increasingly interested. "I see. And you're certain about this connection…? No, I understand the implications… Yes, we can meet tomorrow morning. The cottage is about thirty minutes from your office… We'll be there."

As he ended the call, Mallory gave him a questioning look. "So much for nothing to investigate?"

"There's been a development in the case," Tucker explained. "Santos wants to discuss it in person rather than over the phone."

"How mysterious," Mallory commented, setting down her wineglass. "Did he give you any hints?"

"Just that they've discovered additional evidence while processing the hotel archives," Tucker replied. "Something that connects the Harrington case to other historical events in the region."

"Well, I suppose one meeting won't completely derail our honeymoon," Mallory said. "And I'll admit, I'm curious about what they've found."

They sat together in silence for a few moments, then, as darkness fell, they retreated indoors. The cottage was cozy, with a small living area, a kitchenette, and a bedroom all decorated in soothing coastal colors. After preparing a simple dinner, they settled on the couch to watch a movie.

Around ten o'clock, they went to bed, both pleasantly tired from their day in the sun, and made love. Ten minutes later, Tucker had fallen asleep, but Mallory found herself restless, her mind still processing aspects of the Harrington despite her best efforts to set it aside.

She had finally drifted off, but hadn't been asleep more than twenty minutes when a faint sound from the living room jolted her awake, the subtle creak of floorboards that didn't come from the natural settling of the old cottage. Someone was moving around inside their rental.

Mallory lay perfectly still, listening intently. Tucker continued sleeping soundly beside her, his breathing deep and regular. Another soft creak confirmed her suspicion. Someone was definitely inside the cottage.

Mallory slipped from the bed, reaching for her phone on the nightstand. Not finding it in its usual place sent a jolt of alarm through her; she always kept it charging beside the bed. Someone had moved it.

The bedroom door stood ajar, though Mallory distinctly remembered closing it before going to bed. She glanced around for something she could use as a weapon, settling on a heavy metal statue of a mermaid from the sideboard. She gripped it firmly by its head and, with her heart in her mouth, tiptoed toward the door.

Through the narrow opening, she could see a shadowy figure moving in the darkened living room. The intruder was searching through their belongings, opening drawers and examining the contents of their bags by the beam of a small penlight.

Mallory considered waking Tucker, but hesitated. Any noise might alert the intruder. Instead, she positioned herself behind the partially open door, ready to use the element of surprise if necessary.

The intruder finished with their bags and moved toward the kitchen area, where Mallory and Tucker had left their case notes on the Harrington investigation. The figure—tall, dressed in dark clothing with a face obscured by a ski mask —began photographing the documents with a small camera.

Mallory tensed, weighing her options. The intruder didn't appear armed, but that didn't mean they weren't dangerous. As she prepared to make a move, the floor beneath her creaked.

The intruder spun around instantly, the penlight beam sweeping toward the bedroom door. With her cover blown, Mallory pushed the door open and, wielding the statue, stepped into the living room.

"Don't move," she snapped, her voice firm despite her racing heart. "Who are you, and what do you want?"

The intruder froze momentarily, then spoke in a deliberately muffled voice. "The Harrington case. It's over and done with. Now, for your own sake, you need to leave it alone."

"That's not going to happen," Mallory replied, maintaining her defensive stance. "We don't respond well to threats."

"That's what I thought." The intruder remained unnervingly still. "Have it your way, in which case, I come with a message. Listen to me. You think you know it all, but you don't. There's a journal. It's not in the post, or the cave."

"Journal?" Mallory asked. "What journal? What are you talking about? And why tell me about it?"

"It's hidden where only water meets light," the figure said.

Mallory frowned, surprised by this unexpected information. "What are you talking about? Who sent you?"

"The lighthouse keeper knows," the intruder continued, seemingly working from some kind of script. "Where shadow meets stone at the final alignment. Beware the guardian. Blood protects blood."

Then, before Mallory could respond, the intruder suddenly turned and dashed toward the front door.

"Tucker!" Mallory called out, finally raising the alarm as the intruder pulled open the door.

Tucker, wide-eyed and barely awake, rushed into the room, but by then the intruder was already out the door and sprinting into the darkness.

Tucker reached Mallory's side. "Are you alright? What happened?" he asked, scanning the room for signs of danger.

"We've had a break-in," Mallory replied tersely. "Someone, a man, I think, was searching our things and photographing our case notes."

Tucker moved quickly to the front door, peering out into the darkness, but there was no sign of the intruder. Whoever it was had disappeared.

Closing and locking the door, Tucker turned to Mallory. "Did you see who it was? Did they take anything?"

"I couldn't see their face. He or she was wearing a ski mask," Mallory said, setting the statue down on the dining table. "And I don't think they were here to steal. They said they were here to deliver a message."

As they checked the cottage for signs of forced entry, they discovered the bathroom window had been jimmied open. A clean, professional job. An inventory of their belongings revealed nothing missing, but Mallory's phone had been moved from the bedroom to the coffee table, and a book on the counter—a tourist guide to St. Augustine they had purchased upon arrival—had been opened to a page featuring the St. Augustine Lighthouse. The lighthouse image had been circled in red ink.

"Is this the message?" Tucker wondered, examining the page. "It looks like someone is steering us toward the lighthouse."

"And they mentioned a journal hidden 'where water meets light,'" Mallory added. "Plus something about a lighthouse keeper and 'where shadow meets stone' and a 'final alignment.'"

They checked the doors and windows, securing them as best they could for the rest of the night. Tucker found a chair to wedge under the front doorknob, while Mallory positioned the statue where she could reach it quickly if needed.

"We should call Santos," Tucker said as they finished securing the cottage.

"In the morning," Mallory said. "The intruder is long gone, and we're not in immediate danger. We'd better get some rest and approach this fresh tomorrow. It seems the case is not yet over."

As they returned to bed, both now fully alert and wary, Tucker voiced what they were both thinking. "Someone is worried about what else we might discover."

"And went to considerable lengths to both warn us off and yet point us in a specific direction," Mallory agreed. "It makes no sense. Why would they warn us off, then..." She shook her head. "It makes no sense at all," she muttered, then, "The question now becomes, are they trying to help us solve the case or leading us into a trap?"

Sleep came reluctantly for both of them this time, their senses fully reawakened by the intrusion. The cryptic message echoed in Mallory's mind: "Beware the guardian. Blood protects blood." Whatever secrets remained in the Harrington case, someone was clearly willing to take extreme measures to control how and when they were revealed.

Morning would bring a conversation with Santos, a visit to the lighthouse, and the next chapter in a mystery that refused to let them enjoy their honeymoon in peace. But as disturbing as the night's events had been, Mallory couldn't deny the familiar thrill of the pursuit, the thrill that energized her whenever a case took an unexpected turn. Tucker, she knew, felt the same. It was what had drawn them together in the first place, this shared passion for uncovering truth no matter how deeply it might be buried.

"There's never a dull moment, is there?" she murmured as dawn began to lighten the sky outside their window.

"Would you have it any other way?" Tucker replied with a small smile.

Despite everything, she wouldn't. Their honeymoon

might not be conventionally romantic, but it was undeniably and uniquely theirs: as unpredictable and exhilarating as was their partnership.

17

THE MISSING WITNESS

THE MORNING AFTER THE BREAK-IN, TUCKER AND MALLORY awoke early despite their disrupted sleep. As they prepared for their meeting with Santos, they discussed the implications of the previous night's intrusion.

"This was no random burglar," Tucker said as he re-examined the bathroom window where the lock had been cleanly bypassed. "This guy... or woman, knew what they were doing."

"But how did they know where we were? " Mallory said. "Very few people knew we'd rented this cottage."

Tucker merely shook his head and sighed. "We need to call Santos and tell him what happened. We should have done it last night."

"We would have gotten no sleep at all," Mallory replied. "Let's eat first, then call him."

Tucker stared at her, opened his mouth to speak, then closed it again and shook his head. "Whatever you say, Mal, but we should have called him last night."

They ate a hasty breakfast of waffles from the freezer, then Tucker called him.

"Stay where you are," the detective said. "I'll come to you instead. I want to see for myself."

Santos arrived forty minutes later in an unmarked police cruiser with two forensic technicians following in a separate vehicle. After a thorough examination of the scene, collecting fingerprints and photographing the jimmied window, Santos joined Tucker and Mallory on the cottage's small deck.

"Professional," he confirmed. "No prints on any surfaces—"

"Whoever it was, was wearing gloves," Mallory said, interrupting him.

"Law enforcement training, you think?" Tucker asked, thinking of his own FBI background.

"Possibly," Santos agreed. "Or military. Or private security." He flipped through his notes from their phone conversation. "You mentioned they said something about 'water meeting light' and a lighthouse keeper?"

Mallory nodded, recounting the intruder's specific words. "They said they were delivering a message, a warning" she closed her eyes and thought for a moment, then continued, "They said the Harrington case was over and done with, and that we needed to leave it alone. Then they mentioned a journal and said, 'Not in the post. Not in the cave. Hidden where only water meets light.' Then something about 'the lighthouse keeper knows' and a 'final alignment.'"

"That's weird," Santos said, frowning. "And they deliberately left your St. Augustine guidebook open to the lighthouse page," Santos added. "Someone wants you to go there."

"But why?" Tucker said. "Is someone trying to help the investigation or lead us into a trap?"

"Either way, I think it's connected to Francisco Ruiz's disappearance," Santos replied grimly. "Which is what I wanted to discuss with you this morning."

"Ruiz is missing?" Mallory asked, immediately on the alert.

Santos nodded. "He checked out of the hospital two days ago, seemingly in good health. He told the nursing staff he was going to stay with family in Miami while recovering. But when we tried to contact him for additional testimony yesterday, his family reported they hadn't seen or heard from him."

"Could he have gone somewhere else?" Tucker suggested. "Perhaps he didn't want to be found."

"It's possible," Santos acknowledged. "But his vehicle was discovered this morning, parked in the lighthouse staff lot, but there was no sign of him in the surrounding area."

Tucker and Mallory exchanged a glance. The connection to their midnight intruder's message was too clear to be coincidental.

"The intruder mentioned a lighthouse keeper," Mallory recalled. "They could have been referring to Ruiz rather than the actual lighthouse staff?"

"Ruiz has family connections to the lighthouse through Keeper Andreu," Santos confirmed. "They're distant relatives. And given his knowledge of Timucua history and the artifacts, he might have been investigating on his own."

"And someone wanted us to know where to look for him," Tucker concluded. "Or for whatever he might have discovered there."

Santos' phone rang, and he stepped away to take the call. When he returned, his expression had grown more concerned.

"That was my officers at the lighthouse. They've found evidence of a forced entry at the keeper's quarters. Someone broke in there last night."

"Could it have been the same person who broke in here?" Mallory asked.

Santos shrugged. "It's possible," he replied. "The light-house break-in appears to have happened between midnight and 3 AM, based on security system data. The system recorded a brief power outage that reset the alarms, creating a window of opportunity."

"Again, whoever it was knew what they were doing," Tucker said.

"We need to go to the lighthouse," Mallory said. "Whether Ruiz went there voluntarily or was taken there, it's clearly connected to both his disappearance and our midnight visitor."

"I'll arrange it," Santos said, nodding. "But I can't go. Not yet. I have to wrap things up here, then go back to the station."

He took out his phone and made the call.

THE ST. Augustine Lighthouse stood sentinel at the northern tip of Anastasia Island, its distinctive black and white spiral pattern visible for miles across the water. Built in 1874, the 165-foot tower had guided ships safely through treacherous coastal waters for nearly 150 years.

A young woman in the uniform of the St. Augustine Lighthouse & Maritime Museum greeted them at the visitor center. "Detective Santos called ahead about your visit. I'll take you to Lauren Winters, the assistant director."

Winters was in her office. As they entered, she came around her desk and shook their hands. "Mr. and Mrs. Randall; I'm Lauren Winters. Detective Santos said you were coming. Welcome. How can I help you? "

"Thank you," Tucker said. "We understand you had a break in last night."

She nodded, "That's right. Someone broke into the old

lighthouse keeper's quarters. But as I told the police, as far as I can tell, nothing is missing."

"Did your security cameras capture anything?" Mallory asked.

"That's one of the strange things," Lauren replied, lowering her voice slightly. "We've been having electrical issues all week. The security system was offline between 11 PM and 4 AM last night."

"These electrical issues," Tucker said, "did they affect the other systems besides security?"

"Everything," Lauren said. "Lights, the temperature control malfunctioned, even our point-of-sale computers crashing. Our maintenance team can't find the source. They've checked the wiring, circuit breakers, everything. It's alright now but..." she trailed off.

"Has anything like this happened before?"

Lauren hesitated. "We've had outages, yes, but nothing like this..." She hesitated, then said, "And there have been other... unexplained occurrences reported over the years, especially around certain anniversaries."

"What anniversaries?" Tucker asked.

"Various tragedies associated with the site," Lauren explained. "Construction accidents during the 1874 building, the original lighthouse keeper's mysterious death in 1896, and of course, the incidents with the Timucua artifacts."

Tucker and Mallory exchanged a glance. "What incidents?" Mallory asked.

Lauren looked surprised. "I assumed that's why you were interested in the lighthouse. In 1895, several artifacts believed to be of Timucua origin were discovered during maintenance work on the lighthouse foundation. The keeper at that time, Joseph Andreu, claimed they had been hidden there by his grandfather, who had rescued them from a burial ground that was being destroyed for development."

"The Harrington property?" Tucker asked.

Lauren nodded. "Local legend has it that the hotel is built on a Timucua burial ground, though the historical records are conveniently incomplete. What is documented is that shortly after the discovery, Keeper Andreu disappeared for three days. When he returned, the artifacts were gone, and he refused to discuss what had happened to them. A week later, he was found dead at the base of the tower. His death was ruled an accident, though there were rumors of foul play."

"And this happened in February?" Mallory guessed, thinking of the alignment dates and Isabella Cruz's murder.

"February 16, 1985," Lauren said. "Exactly forty years before the most recent... disturbances."

The dates aligned precisely with the pattern they had been tracking. Forty-year intervals connected to the celestial alignment that had revealed the newel post's hidden compartment. 1895, 1945, 1985, and now 2025, each date marking a death or disappearance connected to the Harrington secret.

"We'd like to see where Keeper Andreu reported finding the artifacts," Tucker requested. "And any areas of the light-house not typically shown to visitors."

Lauren led them first through the keeper's house, a well-preserved Victorian structure that now housed museum exhibits detailing lighthouse operations and maritime history. Beyond the public areas, she unlocked a door marked "Staff Only" that led to a narrow passageway connecting the house to the base of the tower.

"The original foundation stones are visible in this section," she explained, indicating the rough coquina blocks that formed the lighthouse's base. "According to Keeper Andreu's journal, the artifacts were found behind a loose stone in the northeast corner."

Tucker examined the area carefully. "Has anyone

searched here recently? Since Ruiz's disappearance? I understand his car was found here."

"Yes, in the staff parking area, which is strange since he doesn't work here," she replied. "The police did a quick sweep this morning, but they didn't find anything and, as I said, I don't think anything is missing."

Mallory ran her hands along the ancient stonework, feeling for any irregularities. "The message mentioned 'where water meets light.' Could that be referring to this location? The lighthouse guiding ships through water?"

"Possibly," Tucker mused. "Or perhaps more literally..." He directed his flashlight toward the floor, where a thin film of moisture had accumulated in one corner. "Water seepage. Not unusual in a structure this old, especially one built so close to the ocean."

They followed the moisture to its source—a hairline crack in the foundation that widened slightly at floor level. Tucker crouched down, examining it closely.

"There's a draft coming through here," he said. "And it looks like someone..." He trailed off, reaching into his pocket for his pocketknife.

Tucker opened the knife and carefully probed the crack, finding that one of the stones moved slightly under pressure and, with no little effort, he managed to shift it enough to reveal a small cavity behind; not large enough for a person, but sufficiently large enough to hide a moderately sized object.

"Empty," he reported after shining his light inside. "But someone's accessed this hidey-hole recently."

"So you think Ruiz might have come here to retrieve something hidden in this spot?" Mallory said.

"Either Ruiz or someone else got here first, or both," Tucker muttered. "Let's check the tower itself before drawing conclusions."

Lauren led them on along the passageway to the light-house tower entrance. "It's quite a climb to the top," she said. "Two-hundred-nineteen steps, to be precise. The structure itself is original, though it's been renovated several times. We normally don't allow visitors in after hours, but Detective Santos was quite insistent about granting you full access."

"Has anyone else requested special access recently?" Mallory asked as they began the ascent.

"Actually, yes," Lauren replied. "A woman came by yesterday afternoon, claiming to be researching a book about lighthouse history. She was particularly interested in Keeper Andreu and the Timucua artifacts."

"Cordelia Winters?" Mallory asked.

Lauren turned to look at her, frowning. "Yes. How did you know?"

Mallory smiled at her. "Let's just say we've run into her before... Winters, that's your name, isn't it?"

"Yes, but she's no relation to me, though we joked about it. She spent about an hour here, mostly in the archives room, reviewing Keeper Andreu's journals."

Another piece clicked into place; Cordelia's literary interest in the Harrington mystery extended beyond the hotel itself, encompassing this connected historical site as well. Whether her involvement was innocent research or something more calculated remained to be seen.

The spiral staircase wound upward, the metal steps echoing with their footfalls as they climbed. Halfway up, Lauren indicated a small landing with a metal door set into the tower wall.

"This was the assistant keeper's observation room," she explained, unlocking the door. "Now we use it for storage, but it still has the original logbooks and some of Keeper Andreu's personal effects."

The room was small, barely ten feet square, with shelves

along the walls holding boxes of documents and artifacts. A narrow window provided the only natural light, offering a view of the Atlantic stretching to the horizon.

"I'll give you some privacy to look around," Lauren offered. "The police already searched this room this morning but found nothing. Just call if you need anything."

Once alone, Tucker and Mallory began a methodical examination of the room's contents. The boxes held mostly mundane items—maintenance records, visitor logs, financial ledgers—spanning decades of lighthouse operations, but nothing connected to Timucua artifacts.

"This feels like a dead end," Mallory said after twenty minutes of searching. "Maybe we should continue to the top."

As she turned to leave, Tucker noticed something odd about the room's dimensions. "Wait," he said, measuring the space with his eyes. "This room is shorter than it should be, given the tower's circumference."

He moved to the back wall, rapping his knuckles against the painted plaster. The sound confirmed his suspicion. "It's hollow," he said.

Together, they examined the wall carefully. It was Mallory who found it, a small depression near the floor that, when pressed, released a hidden catch. The false wall slid sideways with a grinding noise, revealing a narrow space behind.

What they found within was not ancient artifacts, but more evidence that someone had been there recently. A battery-powered lantern sat on the floor beside a bedroll, a small cooler and several empty water bottles and food wrappers.

"This must be where Ruiz has been hiding," Tucker said, examining the sparse belongings. "But why? And where is he now?"

Mallory picked up a notebook that had been partially concealed under the bedroll. "This might tell us something."

The notebook contained entries in Spanish. Mallory, whose Spanish was basic but serviceable, began translating the most recent entry.

"'February 15, 2025,'" she read. "'I have confirmed what I suspected. The artifacts were never destroyed or lost. They were hidden again by Joseph, my ancestor, when the Harrington men came for them. The location is encoded in the lighthouse plans, exactly where water meets light at the highest point. Tomorrow, during the alignment, I will retrieve them and finally restore what was stolen from our people so long ago.'"

"February 16th," Tucker said. "The same date as the previous incidents in 1895, 1945, and 1985."

"And Keeper Andreu's death," Mallory said grimly.

They continued to the top of the lighthouse, emerging onto the observation platform surrounding the beacon itself. The view was spectacular, with St. Augustine spread out before them to the west and the vast Atlantic to the east. The morning sun cast long shadows across the landscape, including the distinctive silhouette of the Harrington Hotel, just visible in the distance.

"'Where water meets light at the highest point,'" Tucker repeated, scanning the platform for anything unusual. "This is certainly the highest point, but what's the water reference?"

Mallory circled the platform, noting how the light and water intersected from different angles. Then she spotted it, a small metal plate embedded in the floor on the eastern side, directly aligned with the rising sun. The plate was engraved with a compass rose design similar to the one they had found on the map fragment in Room 118.

"Tucker," she called, crouching beside the plate. "Look at this."

The metal appeared newer than the surrounding flooring, suggesting it had been refurbished or replaced. As Tucker examined it, he noticed subtle scratch marks around its edges. "It looks like they beat us to it again," he said. He shook his head, frustrated. "Let's see what's underneath," he said, taking out his pocketknife again.

With some effort, they managed to pry the plate loose, revealing a small cavity beneath. Unlike the empty space in the foundation, this one contained something, a tarnished metal tube about twelve inches long, sealed at both ends.

Tucker carefully removed it, noting its considerable weight. "A document case, perhaps? Or a container for smaller artifacts?"

Before they could open it, a voice from the stairwell interrupted their discovery.

"I'll take that."

They turned to find Cordelia Winters standing at the top of the stairs, a small pistol held in her hand. Her usual elegant appearance had been replaced by practical outdoor clothing, and her expression was hard, determined.

"Cordelia," Mallory said quietly. "What's going on?"

"A correction of historical injustice," Cordelia replied. "Those artifacts belong to my family, the true descendants of the Timucua people whose burial ground Thomas Harrington destroyed. Francisco understood that. He is my cousin, which is why he agreed to help me retrieve them. But then he... he reneged."

"Where is Ruiz now?" Tucker asked, still holding the metal tube.

"Safe," Cordelia assured them. "Once he revealed the location of the hiding place, I no longer needed his help. He's been temporarily... contained while I complete what my ancestors started."

"The intruder in our cottage," Mallory said. "That was you, wasn't it?"

A smile flickered across Cordelia's face. "Simple theatrics designed to lead you here, to help me locate what Francisco was no longer willing to reveal."

"Why involve us at all?" Tucker asked, subtly adjusting his position to place himself between Cordelia's gun and Mallory. "Why not just force Ruiz to tell you everything?"

"Because despite our family connection, Francisco didn't fully trust me," Cordelia admitted. "He knew the artifacts were hidden here somewhere, but not exactly where. I needed your investigative skills to find them. And now you have." She gestured with the gun. "The tube, if you please."

Tucker quickly weighed their options. They were trapped on the lighthouse platform with limited maneuverability. Cordelia stood between them and the only exit, armed and clearly determined. Compliance seemed the safest immediate choice.

"No one needs to get hurt," he said, slowly extending the tube toward her. "But you should know the police are already investigating Ruiz's disappearance. They'll be looking for both of you."

"By the time they figure it out, I'll be long gone," Cordelia replied, reaching for the tube with her free hand. "And you two will have another fascinating case to add to your resume."

As her fingers closed around the metal container, a sudden gust of wind swept across the platform and struck them with enough force to make them all stumble.

Tucker, who'd been holding onto the rail with his free hand, recovered almost instantly. He lunged forward, grabbed her wrist, and forced the gun upward so that it discharged harmlessly into the air. Mallory moved almost as quickly as Tucker, grabbing the metal tube as it fell from Cordelia's grasp.

The struggle was brief but intense. Despite Cordelia's determined resistance, Tucker's FBI training gave him the advantage and, within moments, he had disarmed and restrained her.

"Whew, that was close," Mallory said. "That wind..."

"Let's get her downstairs," Tucker said, securing Cordelia's hands with his belt. "And find out where she's keeping Ruiz."

18

THE OLD REGISTRY

Detective Santos arrived at the lighthouse within twenty minutes of Tucker's call, bringing two officers with him who took Cordelia into custody. Her composure had cracked during the wait, her literary eloquence giving way to bitter recriminations about historical injustice and her right to reclaim her heritage.

"Where's Francisco Ruiz?" Santos demanded after the officers had secured Cordelia in a police vehicle.

"She won't say," Tucker reported. "Just keeps insisting he's 'safe' and 'unharmed.'"

"We'll need to search her residence and vehicle immediately," Santos said. "Given the pattern of escalation in this case, I'm not taking any chances with Ruiz's safety."

While the detective organized the search effort, Tucker and Mallory examined the metal tube they'd recovered. Approximately twelve inches long and three inches in diameter, it was sealed at both ends with caps that had fused with the body over time, requiring careful handling to open without damaging the contents.

"We should wait for proper conservation tools," Santos

advised, returning from his call. "If this contains historical documents or artifacts, improper handling could cause irreparable damage."

"Agreed," Tucker said. "But given the urgency of finding Ruiz, perhaps we should at least confirm what we're dealing with."

Santos considered this for a moment, then nodded. "We have a document specialist at the station who handles evidence preservation. We'll have her open it."

They carefully placed the tube in an evidence container, then followed Santos back to the police station.

While the search for Ruiz continued, they gathered in a small laboratory where a white-haired woman in a lab coat waited.

"Dr. Eleanor Martinez," Santos introduced her. "Our resident expert in historical document preservation. Dr. Martinez, these are the private investigators I mentioned, Tucker and Mallory Randall."

"A pleasure," the specialist nodded, her attention already focused on the container. "Detective Santos briefed me about the potential significance of this find. Let's see what we're dealing with."

Martinez examined the tube under a magnifying light, noting the material composition and corrosion patterns. "Bronze," she said. "Likely late 19th century based on the patina. The seals appear to be lead, which explains their fusion to the body over time."

Using specialized tools, she carefully broke the seal on one end, then extracted the contents with cotton-gloved hands; a rolled document, protected by an outer layer of oilskin that had preserved it remarkably well despite its age.

"It's in excellent condition," Dr. Martinez murmured, gently unfolding the oilskin wrapper.

Inside the protective layer were several items: a folded

parchment document with faded ink writing, a small leather pouch, and what appeared to be a hand-drawn map on yellowed paper.

"Let's start with the document," Dr. Martinez said, carefully unfolding it and placing it under a protective glass screen. "This appears to be in Spanish, though the handwriting style makes it challenging to decipher."

Mallory leaned closer, her limited Spanish strained by the archaic writing style. "It's a letter or statement," she said after a moment. "Dated 1842, from someone named Miguel Antón."

Dr. Martinez nodded, adjusting her glasses as she studied the text. "Miguel Antón was documented as one of the last traditionally educated Timucua descendants in the St. Augustine area. He served as a cultural bridge between the indigenous and the European-dominated society of nineteenth-century Florida."

"What does the document say?" Tucker asked.

"It appears to be a formal protest," Dr. Martinez translated slowly, "against the sale of sacred burial grounds to Thomas Harrington. Antón claims the sale was illegitimate because the land had been designated as protected in earlier Spanish colonial records, a designation that should have carried forward under American administration."

"So Thomas Harrington's acquisition was legally questionable from the beginning," Santos said.

"More than questionable," Dr. Martinez continued, scanning further down the document. "Antón specifically accuses Harrington of bribing officials to alter land records and ignoring indigenous claims. He states sacred artifacts were removed from the burial ground by Timucua descendants before Harrington began construction, to prevent their desecration."

"The artifacts Keeper Andreu claimed to have hidden in

the lighthouse," Tucker said. "His great-grandfather must have been among those who rescued them."

Dr. Martinez carefully unfolded the map next. "This appears to show the original burial ground layout, with markers indicating where specific items were interred. And here—" she pointed to notations along the edge, "—are coordinates corresponding to where those items were relocated after removal."

"The lighthouse location is marked," Mallory said, indicating a symbol near the coast. "But there are other markers as well, scattered throughout the region."

"It looks like they distributed the artifacts to multiple hiding places," Tucker said.

Finally, Dr. Martinez opened the small leather pouch, revealing its contents: a polished stone amulet carved with intricate symbols, a small gold medallion bearing Spanish colonial markings, and what appeared to be a human tooth with a gold filling.

"These would be authentication tokens," Dr. Martinez explained. "Items that could prove the legitimacy of any other artifacts found, through matching craftsmanship, materials, and dental characteristics specific to the population."

"So this tube contains proof of Thomas Harrington's illegal acquisition of sacred land," Santos said, "along with evidence authenticating the removed artifacts and a map to their hiding places."

"And ultimately connects to Captain James Harrington's later crimes," Tucker said. "The son following the father's example of theft and deception, expanding from land to shipwreck salvage."

"A family tradition of misappropriation," Mallory said grimly.

While Dr. Martinez continued her careful examination of

the documents, Santos received a call that pulled him away briefly. When he returned, his expression had shifted from scholarly interest to urgent concern.

"We think we've found Ruiz's location," he announced. "Cell phone triangulation puts Cordelia's phone at a boat storage facility near the marina for several hours last night. The facility owner confirms she rents a unit there."

"Is Ruiz inside?" Tucker asked, already moving toward the door.

"Unknown, but we're assembling a team now," Santos replied. "I thought you'd want to be there, given your involvement in the case."

They left Dr. Martinez to her preservation work, hurrying to join the officers gathering in the station parking lot. Within minutes, a small convoy departed for the marina, lights flashing but sirens silent to avoid alerting anyone who might be watching Ruiz.

The boat storage facility consisted of rows of large metal units, similar to oversized garages, each capable of housing a vessel up to thirty feet in length. Cordelia's unit was at the far end of the complex, partially obscured by a stand of palm trees.

"No signs of external surveillance or booby traps," reported the tactical officer who had done an initial assessment. "Door is padlocked but not alarmed as far as we can determine."

"Open it," Santos ordered.

The lock was quickly cut, and an officer pulled the rolling door upward to reveal the unit's contents: a 26-foot cabin cruiser on a trailer, its white hull dusty from storage but otherwise well-maintained.

"Check the boat," Santos ordered. "Mr. Ruiz could be inside."

Two officers carefully approached the vessel, one

covering while the other climbed aboard to check the cabin. After a tense moment, a voice called from within.

"We've got him! He's alive!"

Tucker and Mallory followed Santos to the boat, where they found Francisco Ruiz bound to a seat in the cabin, gagged but conscious. Apart from dehydration and minor abrasions from his restraints, he appeared unharmed.

"Cordelia," he said hoarsely after the gag was removed and he'd taken several sips from a water bottle. "She betrayed me. She used our family connection to manipulate me."

"Family connection?" Mallory questioned, helping him stand as officers cut the last of his restraints.

"We are distant cousins," Ruiz explained wearily. "We are both descendants of Miguel Antón and the Timucua people who originally inhabited this area. When she approached me about the artifacts, I believed she shared my desire to see them properly recognized and protected."

"Instead, she planned to take them for herself," Tucker said.

Ruiz nodded. "She became obsessed with the idea that the artifacts belonged to her personally, as 'compensation' for historical wrongs. When I insisted they should go to proper cultural institutions, she..." He gestured to his surroundings with a weak smile. "Decided I needed a timeout."

"And?" Santos asked.

Ruiz shrugged. "Drugged tea," he admitted sheepishly. "An old family recipe she claimed would help me connect with our ancestors. Instead, it connected me with this boat seat for the past eighteen hours."

A paramedic team had arrived to examine Ruiz, confirming that beyond mild dehydration and discomfort, he'd suffered no serious harm. While they treated him, Santos pulled Tucker and Mallory aside.

"This case keeps expanding in unexpected directions," the detective said. "It's getting out of hand. "

"And now we have Cordelia's attempt to claim artifacts removed from the cave and from the original burial grounds," Mallory said. "Different motivations but similar methods: deception, manipulation, and violence when necessary."

"Speaking of which," Santos said, checking his phone, "the forensics team has found something interesting in Judge Kincaid's effects. A torn page from what appears to be the Harrington Hotel's original guest registry, dated 1895."

"The same year Keeper Andreu died at the lighthouse," Tucker noted with interest.

"Exactly," Santos confirmed. "And the registry shows that on February 16, 1895—the day of Andreu's death—someone with the last name 'Santos' checked into the Harrington Hotel."

The implication hung in the air between them. Santos' family name, appearing in the hotel registry on the exact date of a suspicious death connected to the artifacts and the forty-year cycle they had been tracking.

"My mother mentioned that her grandmother had worked at the hotel briefly," Santos said quietly. "But never anything about a family member staying there as a guest, especially not one who could afford such luxury in the 1890s."

"The guest's first name?" Mallory asked.

"That's where it gets interesting," Santos replied. "The page was torn precisely through the first name, leaving only 'Santos' visible. Judge Kincaid must have found it while researching the hotel's history and recognized its significance, but someone—presumably Elaine—prevented him from sharing the discovery."

"Another connection between our families and the

Harrington secrets," Ruiz said, joining their conversation after being cleared by the paramedics. "It seems we're all part of this story, whether or not we like it."

"The old registry might hold more answers," Tucker suggested. "Is it still at the hotel?"

"According to Vivian Harrington, the original hotel registers are kept in a climate-controlled storage room beneath the east wing," Santos informed them. "Part of the hotel's historical archive that Blackwood was cataloging before his death."

"We should examine them," Mallory said. "Especially the entries after and prior to February 16th in 1895, 1945, and 1985. If the forty-year pattern holds true, there may be other connections we haven't discovered yet."

"I'll arrange access," Santos agreed. "Though given recent events, I think we should proceed with caution. These historical revelations have already led to multiple deaths. There's no telling what else might be uncovered, or who might want to prevent such discoveries."

As they helped Ruiz to a waiting ambulance for a precautionary hospital visit, Tucker couldn't help but wonder what other surprises awaited them.

19

FAMILY TIES

THE HARRINGTON HOTEL STOOD SILENT AND EMPTY, A CRIME scene tape stretched across its grand entrance. With Cordelia now in custody, and Elaine Kincaid in custody for her husband's murder, Gregory Marsh deceased, and the stolen artifacts recovered from the cave, the immediate criminal aspects of the case had been resolved. But the historical mysteries connecting the hotel to the lighthouse and the indigenous burial ground remained, drawing Tucker, Mallory, and Detective Santos back to where their investigation had begun.

Vivian Harrington met them at a side entrance, her usually composed demeanor noticeably strained by recent events. "Diego," she greeted Santos with a nod before acknowledging Tucker and Mallory. "I've unlocked the archive room as requested. Will you need anything else?"

"Just privacy and time," Santos replied. "And perhaps your insights, if you're willing to share them. We're trying to understand the connections between your family's history and events at the lighthouse."

Vivian hesitated, then nodded. "I'll help however I can.

Recent revelations about my ancestors have been... distressing, but I prefer truth to... falsehoods."

She led them through the quiet hotel, their footsteps echoing in the hallways, normally bustling with guests and staff. The east wing, where Isabella Cruz had discovered something during renovations forty years earlier, felt empty, as if the building itself were holding its breath.

"The archive room is through here," Vivian said, unlocking a door just down the hall from Room 118. "It's climate-controlled; storage for our most delicate historical items, including the original guest registers dating back to the hotel's opening in 1872."

The room seemed smaller than Tucker remembered, with metal shelving units holding carefully labeled boxes and folders. A central table provided space for examining documents, with specialized lighting designed to minimize damage to aged paper.

"The registers are chronologically organized," Vivian explained, pointing to a section of identical leather-bound volumes. "Each book covers approximately two years of guest registrations. Edwin had been digitizing them as part of our historical preservation program, but he'd only completed up through the 1920s before his death."

"We'll need the volumes covering February 1895, 1945, and 1985," Santos said.

While Vivian located the requested books, Tucker and Mallory surveyed the room's contents. Beyond the registers, the archives contained financial records, architectural plans, and personal correspondence to and from generations of Harringtons. It was a comprehensive record of the family's history and the hotel's operations.

"Here they are," Vivian announced, placing three large leather-bound books on the examination table. "I've marked the pages for February in each volume."

The oldest register showed its age despite careful preservation. Its pages yellowed, and the ink faded. Even so, the handwritten entries remained legible, recording names, dates, room assignments, and payment information for guests who had stayed at the Harrington during its early years.

Santos turned immediately to February 16, 1895—the date that had appeared on the torn page found clutched in Judge Kincaid's hand. The day's entries filled a single page, listing eight guest check-ins, including the partially obscured "Santos" entry at the bottom.

"The first name has been torn away," Santos said, examining the damaged page. "But looking at the room assignment and payment notation, this was clearly someone of means. They took one of the premium suites and paid in advance for a week's stay."

"The handwriting is different for this entry," Mallory said, pointing to subtle differences between the "Santos" registration and the ones above it. "As if someone else recorded it, or it was added later."

"The hotel employed multiple desk clerks even back then," Vivian said. "Though you're right, there is something unusual about that particular entry compared to the others."

Tucker had been examining the page with a magnifying glass from a drawer in the table. "There's a very faint notation in the margin beside the entry," he said. "Looks like 'J.H. request' written in pencil rather than ink."

"J.H. would be James Harrington," Vivian said. "My great-grandfather, who was managing the hotel by that time. His father, Thomas, had retired."

"So James Harrington specifically requested this guest be accommodated," Santos mused. "On the same day that Keeper Andreu died at the lighthouse after allegedly discovering Timucua artifacts,"

"That can't be coincidental," Mallory muttered, rubbing her eyes.

They moved to the 1945 register next, again focusing on February 16th. Among the dozen check-ins listed that day, one name immediately caught Santos' attention.

"Elena Mendez," he read aloud, his expression tightening. "That's my grandmother, though she would have been quite young then, barely twenty."

"Your grandmother stayed at the Harrington?" Tucker asked, surprised.

"Not that I'm aware of," Santos replied, studying the entry with increasing concern. "She never mentioned staying at the Harrington, though she worked here later in life. This would have been before she married my grandfather."

"There's a notation here too," Tucker pointed out. "In the 'special requirements' column: 'V.H. approval required for all services.' V.H. would be…"

"Victor Harrington," Vivian supplied. "My grandfather."

"So both in 1895 and 1945, someone connected to the Santos/Mendez family checked into the Harrington on February 16th," Mallory said, "with special notations from the Harrington family manager at the time."

"And each date coincides with reported disturbances related to the Timucua artifacts," Tucker said. "The light-house keeper's death in 1895, and then something in 1945 that we haven't identified yet."

"The lighthouse records might show something," Santos said. "I can have someone check their maintenance logs for February 1945."

They turned to the 1985 register next. February 16, 1985, showed a busy day with twenty-three check-ins including…

"Isabella Cruz," Santos read aloud, his voice tightening with recognition. "Checking in three days before she was killed."

"But that makes no sense," Mallory said, frowning. "She worked here as a maid. Why would she check in as a guest?"

"She didn't," Gloria Mendez's voice came from the doorway, startling them all. Santos' mother stood there, her uniform impeccable as always, but her expression troubled as she entered the archive room. "I checked her in under false pretenses at the request of Richard Harrington."

"Mother," Santos said, clearly surprised by her appearance. "What are you doing here?"

"Vivian called me," Gloria explained. "She said you were examining the old registers, looking for connections between our families. I realized it was time to tell the complete truth, not just the pieces I've shared over the years."

Vivian nodded confirmation. "Gloria has been part of the Harrington Hotel longer than anyone. If there are answers about what happened in 1985, or connections to earlier events, she would know."

Gloria approached the table, looking down at the register entry for Isabella Cruz. "This was part of a plan we developed—Isabella, Francisco, and I—after she found the documents during the east wing renovations. Documents that revealed the Harrington family's involvement in the death of Keeper Andreu in 1895 and another death in 1945."

"What death in 1945?" Tucker asked.

"A lighthouse maintenance worker named Rafael Santos," Gloria replied, meeting Detective Santos' shocked gaze. "Your great-uncle, Diego. Your grandmother's brother, who disappeared while working at the lighthouse on February 16, 1945. Officially listed as a drowning accident, but the documents Isabella found said otherwise."

Santos paled visibly. "I never knew I had a great-uncle who died at the lighthouse."

"Your grandmother rarely spoke of him," Gloria explained. "Her grief was too great, especially knowing the truth but being unable to prove it. The Harrington family had too much influence locally, just as they had forty years earlier when they silenced Keeper Andreu, and forty years before that when Thomas Harrington first stole the sacred land."

"So every forty years, someone connected to either the Santos/Mendez family or the Timucua descendants confronted the Harringtons about their historical crimes," Tucker said, "and ended up dead or disappeared as a result."

"It was all to do with the alignment, but yes, until 1985," Gloria continued. "when Isabella found evidence that might finally expose the pattern. We developed a plan to document everything, to create a paper trail that couldn't be easily destroyed. She checked in as a guest to access areas of the hotel normally off-limits to staff, searching for additional evidence we believed was hidden in the hotel."

"But she was killed before she could complete the search," Mallory said softly.

Gloria nodded, tears forming in her eyes. "Richard Harrington—Vivian's father—discovered what she was doing. He confronted her near the beach stairs. I don't think he intended to kill her, but in the struggle..." she trailed off, the memory still painful decades later.

"My father?" Vivian whispered, shock clear in her voice. "He murdered Isabella Cruz?"

"He admitted it to me the next day," Gloria said. "Claimed it was an accident and that he'd only meant to frighten her into silence. He offered me money, job security, protection for my family—including Diego, who was just a child then—if I helped cover up what had happened."

"And you agreed?" Santos said, his tone unreadable.

"I had three children to support, no husband, and few employment options as an immigrant with limited education," Gloria replied, meeting her son's gaze steadily. "So yes,

I agreed. It's a decision I've regretted every day for forty years, even as I continued working for the family responsible for three generations of deaths connected to my family."

The room fell silent as they absorbed these revelations. Tucker studied the registers again, seeing them now as more than simple hotel records. They were documentation of a deadly pattern, a forty-year cycle of confrontation and silencing that had claimed multiple lives.

"It's all about the alignment," he said finally.

Mallory nodded. "And Edwin Blackwood wasn't killed because he discovered the captain's confession about Miguel Rojas. He was killed because he was connecting it to these other deaths—Andreu, Rafael Santos, Isabella Cruz. He was building a comprehensive case exposing the family's multi-generational conspiracy. But why kill him? It's all old history."

"It's exactly what Judge Kincaid was doing as well," Santos said. "Until Elaine poisoned him; not to protect the Harrington family, but to ensure she could claim the treasure for herself."

Vivian had been listening in stunned silence, her composed facade crumbling as each new revelation implicated her family more deeply in historical crimes. "I knew nothing of this," she said quietly. "My father never spoke of Isabella's death as anything other than a tragic accident."

Meanwhile, Santos had been examining the 1985 register entry. "There's something else here," he said. "Another guest checked in immediately after Isabella. Francisco Ruiz was in the adjacent room. Was that part of your plan, too?"

Gloria nodded. "Francisco was helping us document everything. He has the strongest connection to the Timucua heritage through his mother's lineage. Isabella found the documents, I provided access to restricted areas, and Francisco connected everything to the indigenous history his family had preserved orally for generations."

"So that's why he was so interested in the lighthouse and the artifacts," Mallory said. "He was continuing the work his cousin had started before her murder."

"And why Cordelia targeted him specifically," Tucker said. "She knew of his family connection to the artifacts through their shared Timucua ancestry, distant as it is."

"Cordelia Winters," Gloria said, her expression hardening. "Another opportunist exploiting historical tragedy for personal gain. She approached Francisco last year, claiming a scholarly interest in documenting Timucua cultural heritage. He trusted her because of their family connection, never suspecting she would resort to violence."

"So what began as legitimate historical research became corrupted by greed and ambition," Santos said. "Cordelia, Elaine, Marsh; they all saw an opportunity for personal enrichment."

A question had been forming in Tucker's mind as these connections unfolded. "Gloria, you mentioned a plan you developed with Isabella and Francisco in 1985. A paper trail that couldn't be easily destroyed. What happened to that documentation after Isabella's death?"

Gloria's expression shifted to one of grim satisfaction. "We created three packets of evidence, each containing copies of everything Isabella had found, along with our own research connecting the deaths in 1895, 1945, and potentially 1985. Francisco hid one packet at the lighthouse, in the same location where the original Timucua artifacts had been concealed. I placed another in a safe deposit box under a false name. And Isabella…"

"Hid the third somewhere in the hotel," Mallory guessed.

Gloria nodded. "In the one place no one would think to

look, so we thought: the old cemetery, in Captain Harrington's own grave."

"That's what Marsh forced Ruiz to reveal," Tucker said.

"Evidence that would destroy the hotel's reputation and expose my family's darkest secrets," Vivian said quietly. "Yet here I am, willingly assisting in its discovery. Perhaps that's the difference between my generation and those that came before me."

20

_____

THE MISSING PIECE

THE REVELATIONS IN THE ARCHIVE ROOM HAD SHIFTED THE investigation's focus from solving the recent murders to understanding their historical context, a tapestry of deception, violence, and silence. While Detective Santos arranged for Francisco Ruiz's formal statement to be taken at the station, Tucker and Mallory remained at the Harrington Hotel, continuing their examination of the historical records with Vivian and Gloria's help.

"There's still something missing," Tucker said, spreading timeline notes across the examination table. "We have the forty-year pattern established—1895, 1945, 1985, and now 2025. We know about Keeper Andreu, Rafael Santos, and Isabella Cruz. But Edwin Blackwood was killed before February 16th, not on the anniversary date itself."

"Because he discovered something that couldn't wait," Mallory said.

Gloria, who had been organizing register volumes back onto their shelves, paused thoughtfully. "Before he died, Edwin mentioned finding references to a journal kept by Thomas Harrington—separate from the business records and correspondence that form most of the family archives. A personal journal where he supposedly documented his true thoughts about the indigenous burial ground and his plans for the property."

"Did Edwin locate this journal?" Tucker asked.

"Not that I know of," Gloria replied. "He believed it might be hidden somewhere in the original structure, the part of the hotel that was Thomas Harrington's private residence before his son expanded it into the current building."

"Where exactly would that be?" Mallory asked, looking to Vivian.

"The central section of the east wing," Vivian explained. "Specifically, the area around what's now the hotel library and adjacent rooms. The original home's foundation stones are still visible in parts of the basement beneath that section."

"The basement," Tucker repeated, remembering Blackwood's notes about structural changes not appearing in any official blueprints. "Is it accessible?"

"There's a service entrance near the east wing stairwell," Vivian said. "It's mainly used for storage and maintenance access now, but the original foundation is still intact down there."

Tucker looked at his watch. It was almost eight o'clock. "It's late," he said. "I suggest we get some sleep and assemble here first thing in the morning at, say... eight."

THOUGH MALLORY SLEPT well that night, Tucker didn't. He tossed and turned, sometimes dreaming, sometimes wide awake with the events of the previous days churning through his mind. Eventually, at around six, he rose, went and made coffee, then woke Mallory. They dressed, had a light breakfast of scrambled eggs and toast, and then made the twenty-minute drive to the Harrington, arriving a little before eight to find the rest of the party waiting for them.

With Vivian leading the way, they left the archive room and headed toward the east wing's service areas. The hotel's emptiness lent an eerie quality to their journey, their footsteps echoing through corridors normally bustling with guests and staff. When they reached the access door to the basement level, Vivian produced a ring of keys, selecting a large brass one that looked significantly older than the others.

"This area hasn't been renovated in decades," she explained, unlocking the heavy door. "We've maintained it for historical preservation, but it's not part of the regular hotel operations."

The stairs beyond descended into dimness, illuminated only by sparse emergency lighting that cast long shadows across stone walls that predated the hotel itself. The air grew noticeably cooler and damper as they descended, carrying the mustiness of a space rarely disturbed.

At the bottom, Vivian located a light switch, illuminating a large open area supported by massive stone pillars. Various hotel items were stored here, extra furniture, decorations for different seasons, maintenance equipment, but around the perimeter, the original rough-hewn foundation stones of Thomas Harrington's home were visible.

"This was the basement of my great-great-grandfather's house," Vivian said, her voice hushed in the cavernous space. "Before the hotel was built, before the family came to prominence in St. Augustine society."

"Where would Thomas Harrington have hidden something personal?" Mallory wondered aloud.

Gloria, who had accompanied them, moved toward the far wall. "When I first started working here as a young woman, the older staff told stories about this basement. They said old Thomas had a private study down here, a place where not even his wife was permitted to enter."

She stopped before a section of wall that appeared identical to the surrounding stonework. "It would have been approximately here, though the entrance was supposedly concealed after his death when James converted the house into the hotel."

Tucker examined the wall carefully, running his fingers along the mortar lines between stones. "The construction is different here," he said. "These stones were reset at some point. They're not part of the original foundation. I think it's a sealed doorway. I wonder…" Tucker trailed off, staring at the stones. "Hmm."

"Can we open it?" Vivian asked.

"I don't see why not," Tucker said, the fingertips of both hands on the wall as he stared up at the ceiling. We'll need some tools: a hammer and a stone chisel, I think. If we can remove the mortar, we can pull the blocks out."

"There should be some of those in the maintenance shop. I'll fetch them," Francisco said. And he turned and ran back up the stairs to return a few moments later with two two-pound lump hammers, five chisels of varying lengths, two pairs of safety glasses, several flashlights and a battery-powered lantern. He handed one of the hammers and a chisel to Tucker, kept the other for himself and, together, they set about removing the mortar from between the stones.

"You think Harrigton's journal will be in there?" Mallory asked, her hands over her ears to protect them against the noise.

Francisco nodded. "Not just his journal, but evidence he couldn't bring himself to destroy yet couldn't risk keeping in his home. Evidence related to the displacement of the Timucua people and the desecration of their burial grounds."

"How do you know that?" Vivian asked.

"My family kept records too," Francisco, hammer and chisel in hand, explained simply. "Not in hotel registers or legal documents where they could be altered or destroyed, but in stories passed down through generations, preserved when written history failed or was deliberately manipulated."

"I've spent my life preserving and protecting the Harrington legacy," Vivian said quietly. "Never imagining it was built on such darkness: the displacement of indigenous people, multiple murders, systematic cover-ups..." She paused, took a deep breath and continued, "Whatever we find in that chamber, if there is indeed a chamber, it needs to be properly documented and acknowledged."

"That's all my family has ever wanted," Francisco told her gently. "Not vengeance or compensation, but acknowledgment of what was taken, who was harmed, and how history was distorted to protect the powerful." Then he turned again to the wall and attacked the mortar between the blocks with a will.

"We should inform Detective Santos," Mallory said.

Tucker looked at her and nodded. She made the call.

SANTOS ARRIVED SOME FORTY MINUTES LATER, JUST AS TUCKER and Ruiz were about to break through the wall.

"Here we go," Tucker said as he dropped his hammer and chisel and grasped the large block around which he'd been working. He wiggled the block back and forth, slowly withdrawing it from the wall. It was no easy task, but eventually, the block fell to the floor with a resounding thump.

"Now," he said, breathlessly, grabbing one of the flashlights, "let's see what we've got."

He directed the flashlight through the opening and peered through.

"What is it?" Mallory asked after a moment of silence. "What can you see?"

"Wonderful things," Tucker said, echoing Howard Carter's words as he peered into Tutankhamun's tomb. Then he turned around and said, "I'm joking. There's what looks like a circular chamber about twenty feet in diameter. We need to remove a couple more blocks. Shouldn't be too difficult now we have the first one out."

Twenty minutes later, he and Ruiz had created an

opening big enough for them to crawl through. As their lights swept the space, the architectural details emerged: brick walls reinforced with coquina stone, a domed ceiling approximately twelve feet high at its center, and small niches set into the walls at regular intervals.

"There," Francisco said, pointing to one of the niches. "See?"

They stepped carefully over to the niche, wherein they found a leather-bound book, several small wooden boxes, and what appeared to be rolled parchment documents secured with faded ribbon.

"Thomas Harrington's journal," Vivian whispered, recognizing the distinctive binding that matched other family books preserved in the hotel archives. "And what else?"

"Documentation," Francisco said. "Records he couldn't bring himself to destroy but couldn't risk keeping in his residence or business files."

Tucker carefully photographed the arrangement before anything was touched or moved. "We need to document everything exactly as we found it," he told the group. "The arrangement itself may have significance."

While Tucker recorded the scene, Santos stood back, trained his phone's flashlight on the artifacts and watched.

With the initial documentation complete, they began the delicate process of examining the items. Mallory carefully opened the journal to reveal the first page.

"'Personal Reflections of Thomas Harrington, commenced January 1842,'" she read aloud. "'Not for family review or business records, but for my own reconciliation with actions taken and choices made.'"

"An admission of guilt?" Tucker asked.

"Maybe," Santos said, turning his attention to one of the wooden boxes. "Let's see what else is here."

The first box contained what appeared to be land transaction documents, their official seals and signatures visibly different from similar documents in public records. The second box held several small personal items: a beaded necklace of indigenous design, several arrowheads, and a carved stone amulet.

"Those are Timucua artifacts," Francisco said, his voice tight with emotion. "Taken from burial sites during the property development, despite Thomas Harrington's public claims that no significant items were found."

The third box proved most revealing. It contained correspondence between Thomas Harrington and local officials, explicitly discussing payments for "discretion regarding land title complexities" and "management of indigenous objections." The documentary evidence of corruption and bribery was obvious, preserved in the officials' own handwriting.

"This is why the chamber needed to remain hidden," Tucker said. "These documents could have destroyed both the Harrington family's reputation and implicated government officials, even after their deaths."

While the others continued examining the documents, Mallory had been carefully proceeding through Thomas Harrington's journal, which proved to be a remarkably candid account of his internal struggles regarding the development of the property.

"Listen to this entry from March 1842," she said, reading from the faded pages. "'The old native man came again today, speaking of sacred ground and ancestral spirits. I had Williams send him away with threats of arrest for trespassing, though the law on whose land this truly is remains conveniently malleable through Judge Peterson's cooperation. I find sleep increasingly difficult as construction uncovers more evidence of extensive burial sites. Williams suggests working at night and disposing of the remains in the bay, which we have done these past three evenings. Even

my substantial payments to city officials would not over-
come the scandal should the true extent of this graveyard be
revealed.'"

Vivian's face had paled as she listened

"Keep reading," Francisco urged Mallory. "Does he
mention the artifacts specifically?"

Mallory carefully turned several more pages, scanning
entries until finding relevant content. "Here, July 1842: 'The
native artifacts continue to surface as foundation work
proceeds. Some items appear quite valuable—gold and silver
of apparent Spanish origin mixed with carved stones and
beadwork of indigenous creation. I have instructed the
workers to bring all such findings directly to me rather than
risk their appearance in town, where questions would
inevitably follow. Peterson assures me the land title is now
unassailable in legal terms, but public sentiment could still
prove problematic should the full truth emerge.'"

"He was collecting the artifacts rather than destroying
them," Tucker said. "Despite ordering the human remains
disposed of in the bay."

"Out of greed or guilt?" Santos wondered aloud.

"Perhaps a little of both," Mallory said, continuing to scan
the journal's pages. "Later entries show his perspective
evolving. October 1842 he says: 'I find myself increasingly
troubled by what we uncovered and subsequently concealed.
While the house nears completion and my investment
promises substantial returns, the knowledge of what lies
beneath weighs heavily. Last night I dreamt of figures rising
from the foundation, their empty eyes accusing. Williams
calls this superstitious nonsense, but I wonder if some debts
can never truly be paid with mere money.'"

"He developed a conscience too late," Francisco said, his
tone measured rather than accusatory. "After the damage was
done."

"But he preserved the evidence rather than destroying it completely," Tucker said. "He created this chamber and kept these records intact."

"Perhaps as insurance," Santos said. "Or perhaps more likely as a delayed confession."

As Mallory continued carefully turning pages, a folded document slipped from between the journal's leaves, a map drawn in faded ink on parchment, showing locations throughout the St. Augustine area marked with symbols that combined Spanish notation with Timucua imagery.

"This appears to be a record of where specific artifacts were re-interred," Francisco said after studying it carefully. "Sacred items removed from the burial ground and hidden throughout the region, including the lighthouse location."

Vivian had been examining the correspondence, her expression increasingly troubled. "These letters implicate not just my great-great-grandfather but several founding families of St. Augustine," she said. "Judges, mayors, business leaders, all conspiring to suppress indigenous land claims and conceal evidence of burial desecration."

"Which explains the multi-generational effort to keep these secrets," Santos said. "The conspiracy extended far beyond the Harrington family."

"And anyone who threatened that coalition faced potentially deadly consequences," Tucker said.

As they continued documenting and examining the chamber's contents, Santos checked his watch with growing concern. "We've been down here for an hour and forty minutes," he said. "We need to decide what to do with these materials."

"Everything should be properly removed, preserved, and documented," Vivian stated firmly. "No more hiding, no more secrets."

"I agree," Francisco said, meeting her gaze with newfound

respect. "These materials belong to history, not just my people's history or your family's, but the real history of this region, with all its complexity and painful truths."

They carefully gathered the journal, documents, and artifact boxes, and Tucker continued photographing each item as it was removed.

One by one, the items were passed carefully through the opening into the basement, and from there transported up the stairs into the hotel for further examination.

22

THE CONFESSION

THE MATERIALS RETRIEVED FROM THE UNDERGROUND chamber were carefully transported to the St. Augustine Historical Society's conservation laboratory where specialists in document preservation and historical artifacts could properly assess, treat, and catalog them. Tucker and Mallory accompanied the items, along with Detective Santos, Francisco Ruiz, and Vivian Harrington, all still physically drained from their early morning exploits, but energized by the significance of their discovery.

Dr. Eleanor Martinez, who had examined the contents of the metal tube from the lighthouse, supervised the initial conservation process. Her team worked methodically, ensuring each document and artifact was properly stabilized before detailed examination was allowed to begin.

"The journal is our highest priority," Dr. Martinez explained, directing her team to prepare a controlled environment for the leather-bound book. "Its contents provide context for everything else we've discovered."

While the conservation work proceeded, Tucker, Mallory,

and the others retreated to the historical society's conference room to debrief and plan their next steps.

"The materials are secure," Santos said after conferring with security personnel he'd stationed at the conservation lab. "And Cordelia Winters remains in custody, with no communication privileges. For the moment, the immediate threat to these discoveries appears to be contained."

"What about the hotel?" Mallory asked, looking at Vivian. "Will you reopen it?"

Vivian hesitated before responding. "Eventually," she replied, "but not immediately. The historical and ethical implications of what we've discovered need to be addressed first. I'm already in contact with indigenous cultural experts and legal advisors to discuss appropriate acknowledgment and potential restitution."

"A significant departure from how your ancestors handled similar situations," Francisco said, though his tone was respectful rather than accusatory.

"Breaking cycles requires we make choices," Vivian replied simply. "I can't change what my family did, but I can choose a different path forward."

As they discussed potential approaches to handling the historical revelations, Dr. Martinez entered the conference room.

"We've stabilized the journal and begun a preliminary review of its contents," she reported. "There's something you all should see immediately."

They followed her back to the conservation lab, where Thomas Harrington's journal now lay open in a controlled environment chamber, its pages visible through the protective glass. The entry Dr. Martinez indicated was dated December 24, 1842, Christmas Eve, nearly nine months after Thomas had begun documenting his actions regarding the indigenous burial grounds.

Mallory leaned closer to the glass enclosure, studying the journal entry. The handwriting was a little faded, and cramped but legible, as if Thomas Harrington had been writing in haste or perhaps under duress.

"December 24, 1842," she read aloud. "Christmas Eve."

Tucker positioned himself beside her, his shoulder brushing against hers as they both peered at the aged document.

"Can you read it for us?" Santos asked from behind them.

Mallory nodded and began to read:

"I can bear this burden no longer. The dreams have increased in both frequency and vivacity. Last night I saw them clearly, the native dead rising from beneath my home's foundation, their accusing eyes following me through rooms built atop their desecrated graves. They speak without words, conveying knowledge of my complicity in destroying not merely their resting places, but the evidence of their very existence in this land.

"Williams says this is mere superstition, the imaginings of a conscience weakened by age, but I know better. There is power in this land that predates our claims to it, power that cannot be purchased or buried or legislated away by corrupt officials. I have secreted evidence of my transgressions in multiple locations, not merely as my confession, but as insurance that the truth shall eventually emerge.

"I have devised a system to reveal these locations in cycles aligned with celestial events significant to the native peoples whose rest I disturbed. Every forty years, when the February alignment occurs, the shadows will reveal the way for those with eyes to see. Let the truth emerge when hearts are prepared to receive it."

Mallory paused, looking up from the journal to meet Tucker's gaze. The implications were clear: Thomas Harrington himself had created the forty-year cycle of revelation, designing architectural features throughout his property that would only align during specific astronomical conditions.

"He built revelation into the very structure of his home," Tucker said, voicing what they were all thinking. "But why forty years?"

Francisco Ruiz spoke up, his voice quiet but firm. "In Timucua tradition, forty years represents the span of spiritual renewal, the time it takes for an injured soul to heal and rejoin the cycle of existence. By choosing this interval, Harrington was acknowledging the spiritual debt he owed to those he had wronged."

"So rather than a conspiracy to maintain secrecy," Santos said, "the forty-year pattern was actually designed to gradually expose the truth."

"But someone perverted his intention," Tucker said. "Each time the alignment approached, someone intervened with violence to prevent the revelations: Keeper Andreu in 1895, Rafael Santos in 1945, Isabella Cruz in 1985..."

"And now Blackwood and the others," Mallory finished. "People were killing to maintain a secret that was actually designed to be revealed."

Dr. Martinez directed their attention to the next page of the journal, where Thomas Harrington's confession continued:

"I have instructed Joseph Andreu, whose grandfather assisted in preserving sacred items before my acquisition of this land, to safeguard certain artifacts at the lighthouse. My son James knows nothing of this arrangement, nor of my other hiding places. I fear his ambitions exceed his moral sensibilities, and he would destroy these evidences rather than risk the family's rising position in society.

"I have also placed a sealed letter with my attorney, Mr. Carrington, with instructions that it be opened upon my death and delivered to Governor Moseley. Whether this instruction will be

honored, I cannot say. The conspiracy of silence I helped create has tentacles reaching into every institution of power in Florida."

Vivian had gone noticeably pale as she listened to her ancestor's words. "He tried to expose his own crimes, but was prevented by his son, my great-grandfather."

"And that pattern continued through subsequent generations," Francisco said. "Each Harrington heir choosing family legacy over historical truth."

"Until now," Tucker said, giving Vivian a respectful nod.

Dr. Martinez turned to another document that had been partially stabilized, a folded parchment that had been stored alongside the journal. "This appears to be a map of St. Augustine as it existed in the 1840s," she explained, "with markings at specific locations throughout the property and surrounding areas."

"Marking his hiding places," Mallory said, studying the faded ink carefully. "Look at these symbols, they correspond to celestial positions during specific times of year."

"The cemetery where Captain Harrington was eventually buried is marked," Francisco said, pointing to a symbol near what was now the old family plot. "As is the lighthouse, and several other locations that would have been significant in Timucua spiritual geography."

"So he distributed evidence and artifacts in multiple sites," Tucker said thoughtfully, "ensuring that no single discovery could be easily suppressed."

"But requiring the celestial alignment to reveal their exact locations," Santos added.

As they continued examining the documents, Dr. Martinez's team continued working to stabilize and scan additional pages from the journal. One entry in particular caught Mallory's attention—dated February 15, 1846, just weeks before Thomas Harrington's death.

"I have completed arrangements with Andreu regarding the

artifacts and documentation. The celestial alignment I've calculated will next occur in February 1895, when perhaps wiser minds than those of our current generation might be ready to acknowledge the historical truths without fear of consequence. I have incorporated astronomical markers into the hotel's architecture, the staircase newel post, the east wing window alignments, and the garden pathways. All designed to reveal their secrets only during the specific alignment. Let future generations make better choices than I have."

"He designed an elaborate system of eventual disclosure," Tucker said. "But never lived to see it implemented."

"Because James Harrington found out," Vivian said quietly. "Family letters I've read mentioned that my great-grandfather and his father had a significant falling out shortly before Thomas's death in March 1846. The official cause was listed as heart failure, but..."

"But given what we now know about the family's willingness to eliminate threats," Santos said, "we can't rule out more sinister possibilities."

"The son killing the father to protect the family legacy," Tucker murmured.

"A pattern that continued through generations," Francisco said. "Each time the alignment approached, someone connected to either the artifacts or the historical documentation died."

Mallory had been examining the map more closely. "Look at this," she said, pointing to markings near what would now be the hotel's east wing. "These symbols match those on the fragment we found in Room 118. I think they indicate specific hiding places within the building's structure."

"And this symbol here," Francisco said, indicating a marking at the lighthouse location, "represents 'guardian of truth' in Timucua symbolic language. Keeper Andreu's family must have been entrusted with preserving some of the artifacts and documents."

"Which explains why he was the first to die when the forty-year cycle began," Tucker said.

Santos checked his watch. "I need to update the State Attorney's office on these developments," he said. "The historical significance of these discoveries extends beyond our current murder investigations into potential legal claims regarding land ownership and cultural patrimony."

"I'd like to examine the other locations marked on this map," Tucker said, looking at Vivian. "Starting with Room 118 and the cemetery. There could be additional evidence relevant to both the historical crimes and the recent murders."

"I'll arrange it," Vivian agreed.

As the group prepared to return to the Harrington Hotel, Mallory pulled Tucker aside. "This is bigger than we thought," she said quietly.

"With evidence the original perpetrator actually wanted found," Tucker added. "Just not by his own family."

"Some honeymoon this turned out to be," Mallory said with a small smile.

Tucker returned her smile, taking her hand. "I can think of worse ways to spend our first weeks as husband and wife."

"Only you would say that," she said, squeezing his hand affectionately. "But that's why I married you."

Their moment was interrupted by Dr. Martinez, who approached with another stabilized document. "There's something else you should see," she said, her expression troubled. "A list of names, families who were part of the original conspiracy to suppress indigenous land claims. Some of these names still belong to prominent St. Augustine families."

23

FULL CIRCLE

THE OLD HARRINGTON CEMETERY LOOKED DIFFERENT IN daylight, the moss-draped oak trees less ominous, the weathered headstones less forbidding. With Vivian's permission and Santos' supervision, Tucker and Mallory had returned to examine the location marked on Thomas Harrington's map, accompanied by Francisco Ruiz and an archaeologist from the local historical society.

"This is where we found evidence that someone had accessed a hidden compartment beneath the obelisk," Tucker explained to the archaeologist, a silver-haired woman named Dr. Leona Fisher. "According to the map, there should be more here."

"The original hiding place," Francisco said, studying the cemetery grounds with newfound understanding. "Thomas Harrington began concealing evidence here, before incorporating the revelation mechanisms into the hotel's architecture."

Dr. Fisher circled Captain Harrington's grave slowly, noting subtle differences in the surrounding terrain. "There's definitely been recent activity here," she confirmed, pointing to disturbed soil and vegetation. "But look at this pattern of stone placement around the perimeter of the plot."

The team gathered around as Dr. Fisher indicated a series of small, flat stones set into the ground at regular intervals surrounding the Harrington family plots. Most were partially covered by grass and soil, nearly invisible unless one knew to look for them.

"These aren't random," Dr. Fisher said. "They form a perfect astronomical alignment. During certain celestial events, shadows from the obelisk would fall precisely on these markers, creating a pattern visible only under specific conditions."

"The February alignment again," Mallory said.

"But Marsh already found whatever was hidden beneath the obelisk," Tucker pointed out. "What else could be here?"

Francisco had stepped back, surveying the cemetery from a different perspective. "It's not the individual stones," he blurted. "It's the pattern they create. Come. Look at the overall layout from this angle and don't blink."

The group shifted position, following Francisco's gaze. From their new vantage point, the arrangement of stones, grave markers, and natural features resolved into a recognizable pattern—a celestial map mirroring specific constellations significant in Timucua cosmology.

"The graves themselves are part of the map," Dr. Fisher said, her voice hushed with awe. "The entire cemetery is an astronomical device, designed to reveal something only when viewed from precisely the right position during the alignment."

"And that position would be..." Tucker began, looking around the cemetery grounds.

"The lighthouse," Francisco said confidently. "The highest point with line-of-sight to this location. During the February alignment, the sun's position would create shadows aligning perfectly with this pattern, visible only from that elevation."

"Which explains why Keeper Andreu was at the light-house during the 1895 alignment," Mallory said.

With careful excavation supervised by Dr. Fisher, they began investigating the areas indicated by the celestial map. At three points around the cemetery's perimeter, they discovered small caches concealed beneath marker stones, each containing fragments of documents and small artifacts that, individually, seemed inconsequential but together formed a compelling historical record.

"He dispersed the evidence," Tucker said as they cataloged each discovery. "No single cache contained the complete story, but together they create an undeniable historical record."

The most significant find came from beneath a simple stone at the cemetery's eastern boundary, a metal box similar to the one recovered from the lighthouse, but considerably more weathered. Inside was a document listing payments made to local officials, bribing them to alter land records and suppress indigenous claims to the property.

"This is exactly what subsequent generations of Harring-tons were willing to kill to protect," Dr. Fisher said as she carefully preserved the fragile papers. "This is evidence that the family's entire fortune was built on illegally acquired land and corrupted governmental processes. What that might mean today, though, is anyone's guess."

"Could it be potentially subject to legal challenge even today?" Santos asked. "Given the fraudulent nature of the original transactions."

"I somehow doubt it," Tucker replied. "The statute of limitations must have run out more than a century ago."

"But not the moral implications," Francisco muttered.

As the morning turned into afternoon, the team moved to

the lighthouse, where Cordelia's attempt to recover artifacts had been foiled. With proper archaeological protocols in place, they examined the hidden compartment Tucker and Mallory had discovered. A systematic search revealed a false bottom to the cavity, concealing an additional chamber beneath.

"It's untouched," Dr. Fisher muttered as she carefully removed the layers of materials placed within. "Pottery fragments, shell beads, ceremonial implements. They're all consistent with Timucua traditions dating from before European contact."

Among the artifacts was a brass box, considerably larger than the tube they'd found. Unlike the other items, which had been arranged with obvious ceremonial intent, this appeared to have been added years after the original cache, perhaps during one of the forty-year alignments.

"This doesn't belong with the original artifacts," Dr. Fisher said, carefully retrieving the case. "The metal, the lock and the manufacturer are all consistent with the late Victorian era."

The box's locking mechanism had corroded over time, requiring careful handling to open without damaging its contents. Inside, wrapped in oilcloth that had preserved it remarkably well, lay a leather-bound book along with several folded documents bearing official seals.

"Another journal," Tucker said as Dr. Fisher carefully removed it from its protective wrapping.

The inside cover bore an inscription: "Record of Observations and Actions, 1886-1895, J. Harrington." It was James Harrington's personal account of his activities during the decade leading up to the first alignment after his father's death, culminating in the murder of Keeper Andreu.

A quick examination revealed that the accompanying documents were official police and coroner's reports relating to Andreu's death, with noticeable discrepancies between the draft versions and final signed reports. The differences clearly showed how evidence of foul play had been systematically removed from the official record.

"He documented his own cover-up," Santos said with professional disbelief. "Why preserve evidence of your own crime?"

"The same reason his father created the system of revelation," Francisco suggested. "Conscience. Having killed Andreu to protect the family legacy, perhaps James couldn't bring himself to completely destroy the evidence. Instead, he hid it where it would eventually be found, continuing his father's wishes."

The final pages of James Harrington's journal contained a letter addressed to "Future Generations of Harringtons," explicitly instructing his descendants to continue monitoring the forty-year cycles and to "take whatever measures necessary" to prevent the exposure of the family's founding crimes.

"So it was James who corrupted his father's intention," Mallory said. "Thomas wanted confession and reconciliation, but James transformed it into an ongoing conspiracy of concealment."

"A conspiracy that continued through Victor's actions in 1945 and Richard's in 1985," Tucker added. "Until Vivian finally broke the cycle in 2025."

With the lighthouse cache thoroughly documented, they returned to the hotel, where further examination of Room 118 had yielded additional evidence behind the wall paneling, a comprehensive record of the Harrington family's systematic suppression of indigenous land claims, accompanied by a map showing the original boundaries of the Timucua sacred sites before the advent of European development.

That evening, the team gathered in the hotel parlor to assess their discoveries. The room, normally filled with guests enjoying pre-dinner cocktails, now served as an impromptu conference space for a historical revelation decades in the making.

"What we've uncovered amounts to a comprehensive record of historical crimes and their subsequent cover-up," Santos said. "From Thomas Harrington's original land theft and desecration of indigenous burial grounds to the murders committed by three generations of his descendants to protect the family secret."

"Not to mention the additional crimes committed by Elaine Kincaid and Cordelia Winters in their attempts to capitalize on these revelations," Tucker added.

"The question now," Santos continued, "is how to proceed with this information. There are potential legal implications regarding land ownership, cultural patrimony rights, and, of course, the prosecution of those responsible for the recent murders."

"The artifacts should be returned to appropriate Timucua cultural representatives," Francisco said firmly. "And the historical record should be made publicly available, regardless of how it might affect certain families' reputations."

Vivian nodded her agreement. "I've already contacted my attorneys to establish a foundation dedicated to indigenous cultural preservation and historical truth. The hotel will eventually reopen with a museum documenting both the Timucua history and the Harrington family's complicated legacy."

"A significant departure from how your ancestors handled similar situations," Francisco muttered.

As the meeting concluded and everyone prepared to depart, Santos approached Tucker and Mallory. "I've been authorized to release your cottage from the crime scene restriction," he said. "You're free to resume your honeymoon. What's left of it, anyway."

"Thank you, Detective," Tucker said, shaking Santos' hand. "For your cooperation and your commitment to the truth, despite its complications for your own family history."

"My grandmother would be pleased," Santos replied. "She always believed there was more to both Isabella's death and her brother Rafael's disappearance than the official record showed. Finding the truth after all these years brings its own kind of peace."

———

Two days later, Tucker and Mallory sat on the deck of their rented beach cottage watching the Atlantic waves roll endlessly toward shore. The morning newspaper lay on the table between them, its headline announcing: "HISTORICAL DISCOVERY AT HARRINGTON HOTEL REVEALS CENTURIES OF SECRETS."

"It's going to be quite a legal and historical mess, I think," Tucker said, sipping his coffee. "Land claims, cultural heritage rights, criminal prosecutions for the modern murders..."

"But necessary," Mallory replied.

Her phone buzzed with a text from Santos, updating them on developments. Elaine Kincaid had accepted a plea deal. She confessed to her husband's murder in exchange for a reduced sentence. Cordelia Winters was facing multiple charges related to Francisco's kidnapping and the attempted theft of cultural artifacts, though her legal team was already floating an insanity defense.

"Vivian's foundation is already gaining considerable support," Mallory reported, reading from the text. "Several other prominent St. Augustine families whose ancestors were implicated in the original conspiracy have come forward to contribute funds toward restitution and cultural preservation efforts."

"A better outcome than Thomas Harrington could have hoped for," Tucker said. "Though at a much higher cost in human lives than should have been necessary."

"Full circle," Mallory said thoughtfully. "The February alignment revealed exactly what he intended, just a century and a half later than he planned."

Tucker reached across the table to take her hand, his thumb brushing gently over her wedding band. "So," he said with a small smile, "are you ready to resume our honeymoon now that the case is solved? Or should we search for more historical conspiracies?"

Mallory laughed, the sound carrying across the empty beach. "No. Never. No more. I think we've earned some actual rest," she said. "Though I have to admit, it was a memorable start to married life."

"Life is never boring with you," Tucker said, leaning over to kiss her softly.

And they sat together, hand-in-hand in comfortable silence, watching the endless rhythm of the waves. The tide was coming in, washing away their footprints from an earlier walk along the shore. By tomorrow, no trace of their passage would remain. Tucker squeezed Mallory's hand, and she returned the pressure.

"Home tomorrow," she said. "I'm glad. I miss Annie."

EPILOGUE

SIX MONTHS LATER

THE HARRINGTON HOTEL REOPENED ON A CRISP AUTUMN morning, its Victorian facade freshly painted but subtly altered. The grand entrance now featured a new annex, an elegant glass structure housing the Timucua Cultural Heritage Center that connected seamlessly to the historic building while clearly representing something new.

Tucker and Mallory Randall stood among the invited guests for the ribbon-cutting ceremony, having flown in from Chattanooga at Vivian Harrington's personal request. In the months since the February alignment and its bloody aftermath, they had returned to their normal caseload, their honeymoon adventure fading into a wild but meaningful memory as they settled into married life.

"It's quite a transformation," Tucker commented, surveying the crowd gathered on the hotel's front lawn. Representatives from Timucua cultural organizations stood alongside St. Augustine's political leaders, historians, and several federal officials overseeing the legal resolution of land claims stemming from the revelations.

"Vivian's done an impressive job," Mallory agreed. "Not

many people would want to convert a family scandal into a cultural reconciliation project."

Detective Santos approached, accompanied by his mother, Gloria, and Francisco Ruiz. The family resemblance between mother and son was more apparent now that they stood together, both appearing more at peace than when Tucker and Mallory had first met them.

"The Randalls," Santos greeted them warmly. "It's good to see you both looking so well-rested. No more midnight break-ins, I hope?"

"Our cases since returning home have been refreshingly straightforward," Tucker replied, shaking the detective's hand. "Though Mallory keeps hoping for another historical conspiracy to unravel."

"One was enough," Gloria said firmly, but with a knowing smile.

Francisco nodded in agreement. "Finding the truth after all these years has brought unexpected healing. Not just for our families, but for the broader community."

The community's healing was clear in the gathering before them. Representatives from indigenous groups and academics conversed with local business owners whose establishments had benefited from the renewed interest in St. Augustine's complex history, and tourists waited eagerly for their first glimpse inside the renovated hotel and its new museum.

"Strange to think it all began with Edwin Blackwood's research," Mallory said. "One historian determined to uncover the truth, regardless of the repercussions."

"And he paid for that determination with his life," Santos replied soberly. "As did Chef Dupont and Judge Kincaid. Not to mention those who died in previous cycles: Isabella, Rafael Santos, Keeper Andreu."

"Their deaths weren't in vain," Francisco said. "Each of

them helped preserve pieces of a truth that eventually emerged complete."

A hush fell over the crowd as Vivian Harrington approached the podium set up on the hotel's front steps. Her trademark composure endured, but there was a new quality to her bearing, a genuine humility that had replaced her previous aristocratic reserve.

"Ladies and gentlemen," she began, "welcome to the reopening of the Harrington Hotel and the inaugural day of the Timucua Cultural Heritage Center. This moment represents not merely a new chapter for a historic property, but what I hope will be the beginning of genuine reconciliation for our community."

As Vivian continued her speech, acknowledging both the painful history being commemorated and the steps toward healing already underway, Tucker felt Mallory slip her hand into his.

"You know," she whispered, "we never had a proper honeymoon."

Tucker smiled. "I was thinking the same thing. But I'm not sure St. Augustine would survive another Randall vacation."

"Actually," Mallory said with a mischievous glint in her eye, "I was thinking something more exotic. Cordelia Winters' trial revealed connections to potentially looted artifacts in Greece. I thought perhaps—"

"Don't even go there," Tucker interrupted her, though his smile belied any real objection. "International art theft and archaeological intrigue aren't exactly restful."

"But it might be romantic," Mallory said. "Mediterranean islands, ancient ruins, mysterious collectors..."

"And knowing you, at least one dead body," Tucker said dryly.

"I can't promise there won't be," she admitted. "But isn't that what makes life interesting?"

Tucker's response was interrupted by applause as Vivian concluded her speech and ceremonially cut the ribbon stretched across the hotel's entrance. As guests began filing into the newly renovated lobby, Francisco approached them once more.

"Before you leave," he said, "there's something I've been asked to give you." He handed them a small package wrapped in simple brown paper. "From Gloria. A token of appreciation for your role in bringing the truth to light."

Inside the package, they found a small carved stone amulet, a replica of one recovered from the lighthouse cache, depicting intertwined symbols representing truth and justice in Timucua iconography.

"It's beautiful," Mallory said, turning the piece over in her hand.

"Gloria said it is to be a reminder. " Francisco explained. "She thought you might appreciate the sentiment."

As they toured the new museum later that afternoon, Tucker and Mallory found themselves before a display case containing the metal tube from the lighthouse and the journal discovered in the cemetery. A placard explained their significance in the forty-year cycle of revelation and conceal-ment, crediting "visiting investigators Tucker and Mallory Randall" with helping to uncover the final pieces of the puzzle.

"Look at that," Mallory said with satisfaction. "We're part of the historical record now."

"It's just a footnote," Tucker replied modestly.

"For now," she said, her eyes twinkling with characteristic determination. "But I have a feeling—"

"I said, don't go there," Tucker interrupted her. But the mischievous look on her face told him it was futile. If their honeymoon adventure had taught them anything, it was that life with Mallory would never be predictable, never be boring. Whatever case came next—whether in Chattanooga or Greece or anywhere their investigations might lead—they would face it together, partners at work and in life.

As they left the Harrington Hotel that evening, the setting sun cast long shadows across the grounds, not unlike those that had revealed hidden truths during the February alignment. But unlike those shadows, these were simply the natural play of light at day's end.

"Ready to go home?" Tucker asked as they reached their rental car.

"Home," Mallory repeated, closing her eyes. "Definitely. Yes, but I was thinking—"

"Oh geez," Tucker said, interrupting her. "Here we go again."

THANK you so much for reading, Never No More, the 4th book in the Randall & Carver Mysteries. I hope you enjoyed this story and will share your love for reading with your friends. My complete list of books is on the next page if you are looking for more.

From Blair Howard

The Harry Starke Genesis Series
9 Books in Series as of 2025

The Harry Starke Series
25 Books in Series as of 2025

The Lt. Kate Gazzara Murder Files
21 Books in Series as of 2025

Randall And Carver Mysteries
4 Books in Series as of 2025

The Peacemaker Series
3 Books in Series as of 2025

The O'Sullivan Chronicles: Civil War Series
5 Books in Series as of 2025

From Blair C. Howard

The Sovereign Star Series
7 Books in Series as of 2025

Also available in German

The Predecessors
1 Book in Series as of 2025

ABOUT THE AUTHOR

Blair Howard is a retired journalist turned novelist. He's the author of more than 50 novels including the international best-selling Harry Starke series of detective crime stories, the Lt. Kate Gazzara Police Procedural series, the Harry Starke Genesis series, and the Randall & Carver Mysteries. He's also the author of the Peacemaker series of international spy thrillers and five Civil War/Western novels.

If you enjoy reading Science Fiction thrillers, Mr. Howard has made his debut into the genre with, The Sovereign Stars Series under the name, Blair C. Howard.

www.BlairHowardBooks.com

www.ingramcontent.com/pod-product-compliance
Lightning Source LLC
Chambersburg PA
CBHW011347010726
47493CB00011B/2997

9 7 9 8 9 9 9 8 8 0 2 4 2 3